Watch for More
Novels by Edith Gleason

from Indigo Sea Press

indigoseapress.com

After the Rains

By

Edith S. Gleason

Veracity Books
Published by Indigo Sea Press
Winston-Salem

Veracity Books
Indigo Sea Press
302 Ricks Drive
Winston-Salem, NC 27103

Copyright 2015 by Edith Gleason

First Veracity Books edition published December, 2015

Veracity Books, Moon Sailor, and all production design are trademarks of Indigo Sea Press, used under license.

For information regarding bulk purchases of this book, digital purchase and special discounts, please contact the publisher at *indigoseapress.com*

Cover design by Stacy Castanedo

Manufactured in the United States of America
ISBN 978-1-63066-271-4

I dedicate this book to my mother Maxine Lason, for being such a terrific encouragement.
To my friend Susan Jordan for proofreading.
To my daughter Anna for her help in editing and my daughter Angel for her cover picture. Mostly to my Heavenly Father, That loves me enough to give me the gift off storytelling.

Chapter One

"Zach! Zach!" Angel cried out to her little brother, who was now lying in a crumpled mass at the foot of the rocky hill. "I told you to wait!" She wailed in anguish as she ran to his side. She tenderly lifted the small limp boy. His motionless body was broken; he couldn't hold up his arms, so they fell to his sides. She held him close, calling out his name, as if she could will life back into his small lungs. Try as she may, he lay still in her arms.

Angel began to rock him back and forth, clutching him tightly, unwilling to release him. She sobbed there, squeezing Zach and letting her tears cover his solemn face, until a townsman gently touched her shoulder.

*****

"Rawk, rawk!" The shrill call of a bird pierced through her thoughts and startled Angel awake. She sat up, her hands balled into fists, with her thumbs poking out between her middle and forefingers. She wiped the perspiration from her brow and sighed. Once again she relived a memory that had become a reoccurring nightmare. "What doesn't kill you, dear, makes you stronger," her grandmother had told her once, shortly after that fateful day. Years had passed, and still she didn't feel any stronger. Life continued and the hurt silently lived on. As for redemption, it still had not found her.

Angel brushed the grass from her hair and with the back of her hand wiped her face. The tree she sat beneath provided shade but didn't stop the attack of the heat on this hot summer day. August was always the hottest, especially in the west, as Papa would say, where the sun shines the brightest.

Looking at her surroundings, she couldn't believe that she had fallen asleep during the horse races. Angel looked dreamily over at the cowboys. Ever since she was little, she loved watching the cowboys race their steeds, and one cowboy in particular always caught her eye: Wes.

1

Edith Gleason

Angel thought he had to be the most perfect specimen of a young man she had ever seen. At twenty-two years of age he was a towering six-foot muscled, rugged young man, his thick dark brown hair was always parted to the side. Amusingly, to her it looked like a hat on his head. Beneath his hair, his bright blue eyes twinkled like sparks of light. He had briefly spoken to her before in a greeting and sometimes would nod her way; and when she caught him staring, he would tip his hat and smile. To say that she was taken with him wasn't quite it, just more of a growing curiosity for now.

Today, however, Wes didn't nod or even smile her way; he seemed distracted. Lack of acknowledgement bothered Angel.

"Whoa, you're doing some heavy plotting," Casey noted aloud, interrupting her thoughts as he plopped down on the grassy spot beside Angel. "Hey, this is pretty comfy," he declared. "How'd you get the best seat in the house? Did you pay somebody off?" Casey asked. Casey was her best friend. His dad was a longtime hand on their ranch, so they grew up together. Casey's sandy hair, bright green eyes and freckled face always made him look mischievous, which she had to admit he was. At times she had found him annoying, and this particular moment was one of those times.

"You know very well what I'm doing here. I 'm watching the races," she responded with irritation.

"Sure, how could I forget how much you love the races and not just the cowboy by the name of Wes? Don't bet the farm on him just yet, 'cause I think Billy's gonna beat him today!" he chuckled.

Upset with the conversation, she put her hands on her hips and demanded, "How did you find me, anyways?"

"Your Pa sent me." Casey, it seemed, was always aware of Angel's whereabouts. At least that's the way Angel saw it. Every time she turned around, there he was. He felt the need to protect her (he had told her so), but who was going to protect her from his constant attention?

"Your pa said that it's time we get going, that is, if you want to open your presents and entertain your guest, who will be at your house in less than an hour."

Angel jumped up, "Oh! I can't believe I almost forgot that!"

She stood up quickly, adjusting her petticoats and dress, and brushed herself off, while absently looking over towards Wes and Billy. A thought occurred to her: *Now was just as good a time as any to get his attention.* Leaving Casey in the dust, she gathered up her dress as she hurried toward the horse corral. Without stopping she called over her shoulder to Casey, "Tell Papa I'll meet you at the wagon in a few minutes." Her task was to do some fast talking. Her approach was going to appear a bit unladylike, thanks to the branches that clawed at her dress and slowed her running.

"Don't look now, but I see a young lady headed this way," Billy said, looking up and laughing to himself.

Wes looked up and saw Angel, all but running his way. He smiled.

Angel stumbled. The ground came rushing to her face when a strong arm reached around her waist and stopped her from propelling to the ground. After regaining her composure, she brushed the hair from her eyes to see that it had been Wes who had rescued her.

"Thank you. I'm sorry; these long dresses get in the way sometimes." Angel blushed as she excused herself.

Wes laughed. He didn't think that Angel ever slowed down. Even at eighteen she still had a bit of tomboy in her. He enjoyed her attention; she was not only bright but also easy on the eyes. He had assessed her years ago as a heartbreaker. Her deep blue eyes were clearer than the sky. Her long wavy brown hair flowed about her waist and most times, he noticed, seemed to be a challenge for her to control. Her form was slight, and Wes guessed that if it were not for the layers of clothing, she would be even smaller.

He knew he had to gaze down a ways to look in her face, so he guessed her to be about five-foot-two. He focused again on Angel and steadied her, "Where are you off to in such a hurry, Angel?"

"Actually I was coming here to talk to you. I wanted to know if you were going to stop by the ranch. Mama and Papa are holding a celebration for my birthday, and I'd be delighted if you would attend."

"Today, huh, your pa gave us some fencing to fix out on the range. It appears that the spring rains, along with the mountain's

3

melting snows, did quite a bit of damage. Your father asked us to repair as much as we could today. Of course, he told us to have our fun first. That's why we are at the races."

Wes released Angel, "I'm sorry; unfortunately I cannot attend your party. With a little more notice, maybe next time I'll be able to come. You have a happy birthday, Angel. I'm pleased you took time out to come see the races."

Angel smiled, "That would be nice. Well, Papa's holding the wagon for me. He says it's time to go, but maybe I'll see you later at the ranch."

Wes nodded and tipped his hat to her, then watched as her skirt and petticoats began flying about her as the dutiful daughter took off running.

Chapter Two

"Tell your momma why we're late," Hank softly demanded his daughter, as he nudged her out in front of him.

"I'm sorry, Momma. I was inviting other people to come to the party, but they can't attend. Can you forgive me?" Angel pleaded.

"Always, my darling," Cat cooed to her only daughter. "There is nothing unforgivable when it comes to you. You see, Angel, that's how the Lord loves us. Sometimes we don't forgive ourselves, but God always forgives." Momma reached out and lifted a blade of grass from Angel's hair. "Go make yourself presentable again; you have guests who are waiting."

Caitlyn was lovingly called Cat by all that knew her, mainly because she was so quick at everything she did and also because she was quick-witted. The proof for this was the laughter she could rouse at any given moment from her children and her husband; they were her best audience.

The laughter that boomed from the other room caused Cat to think back to an unhappy time. After she had lost poor little Zachery, she felt sure none of them would ever smile again. However, with God's gentle touch, life is proof that from tragedy is born strength and healing. In her heart, she wished Zachary could have been there today, but she knew he was in a better place and waiting for them. She had observed throughout the years that Angel blamed herself for her little brother's misfortune. Cat had watched and prayed that someday Angel would forgive herself.

Cat loved her family. She had been blessed with only one daughter, and that was Angel. One might say that she was spoiled; Cat pondered that many times. She didn't want her daughter, or for that matter any of her children, to think that life would hand them conveniences or a free ride. Angel was very loving and kind, all because Cat made sure not to give in to her too much. Still, Hank and Cat couldn't deny her any request, and neither could her brothers. "That's why the Lord gave us children: to lavish his love upon them, while he molds them for His glory."

5

Cat would always remind herself of that, especially when she had let a little discipline for the children slip past her. She remembered her mother saying, "You can't put an old man's head on a young child's shoulders." It was now that Cat realized the wisdom in that.

Cat knew she could've had the servants take care of the cooking today, but she refused to let them. She had been taught from an early age that one should never ask anyone to do that which they could do for themselves. It wasn't a matter of not appearing lazy, or a matter of pride, just simply honoring the Lord in everything you do.

She could hear the children hushing and Hank beginning to introduce the special gift they had purchased for their daughter. Listening to him now, she thought with a smile, *he is so dramatic.* Wiping her hands, she hurried into the parlor to be a part of the giving. She didn't want to miss a second of Angel's reaction.

Angel's brothers, Toby, Tim, Andrew and Carson, stood behind Hank as he presented the gift to her. "My little Angel, she's growing up so fast. One of the hardest things for a parent to do is to be apart from their children. So this gift was the hardest one to give you."

Swallowing his tears, Papa continued, "In our everyday lives, your momma always sees a moral in everything that happens. I see a story that needs to be told, and *you* see lessons that need to be taught. You've voiced how much you would love to be a teacher. So much so that even the townsfolk know it," Hank teased. "We've watched over the years as you poured your heart into helping teach the children that couldn't attend school how to read. God knows we need teachers in this town." Hank reached inside his vest pocket and withdrew a large envelope. He held it out for Angel to take.

"These are admittance papers for Boston College, which you'll be attending for the next three years where you'll be taught how to be a teacher. Your mother, your brothers and I all love you very much, Happy birthday, sweetheart." Hank put his arms around his daughter and drew her close.

Angel's eyes had widened and her mouth was agape. She shook as she held the envelope in her hands. Tears of joy slid down her smiling cheeks. "Oh, Momma and Papa, how could I ever thank you enough?" She clutched the envelope tightly to her chest and hugged

6

her family that had gathered around her.

"This is the happiest moment of my life; I'll cherish it always. But someone needs to tell me how I'm going to get along without all of you? I know I'm going to be way out east and miss all of you so much."

"Well, my advice is to just stock up on memories 'cause you won't be leaving for a bit," Tim offered.

"I have a feeling that you'll manage. Just write us when you can and, besides, you'll be home for the holidays. It won't be as long as you think. And remember to do everything as unto the Lord. That in itself will make us proud," Momma reminded her.

Angel stood by herself for a few minutes, clutching and contemplating her gift. A soft whisper against her ear reminded her of where the need to teach came from; it was from the tragedy of her younger brother. Even now she knew that there was nothing she could've done to save Zachery but still could not forgive herself. Back then she found comfort in knowing there were other children she could help, maybe not in the same way, but in another way.

A quick breeze touched a strand of her hair and lifted it against her face. She smiled as she touched her cheek, then whispered, "I love you too, Zach." Angel, lost in thought, now lifted her head and answered, "I will, Momma." Angel smiled, "Everything as unto the Lord." She had been reared by Momma's wisdom and grew to accept it. Her friends were laughing nearby and teasing her with stories from her childhood as she opened the rest of her gifts. While Angel was cleaning up the wrappings and dishes, a friend approached.

"Angel, you must know that I will certainly miss you the most," Langley said, standing next to her. He was the son of the richest land baron in all of Montana. Their land surrounded Papa's ranch.

He was spoiled and a bit snobbish. In spite of that, Angel had thought that he stood out in a crowd since he was good-looking. Langley stood straight with his shoulders back. He wasn't very tall, but he had a solid build. He had brown eyes and blond hair. The only thing that ruined him, in her opinion, was his lack of personality. She put up with his attentions and even enjoyed them sometimes, but she still didn't regard him as anything further than an acquaintance.

"Papa says three years isn't that long. You'll be going to school too, I hear. Will it be one around here?"

"No, I'll be traveling to a different state; but, yes, I'll be attending Business College. Father wants me to run his ranch and learn his business affairs and then later, when he feels I'm qualified, take over his duties."

"Well, I'm sure you can handle it. You seem to have a real knack for business."

"Yes, my father has been training me every chance he gets. He says I was born for it, like a horse straight out of the gate." Then his voice turned formal, "I've enjoyed myself here, but it's time for me to be leaving. Have a wonderful birthday, Angel, and thank you for inviting me. Before I go," he reached inside his breast pocket, "here. It's a gift I picked out especially for you." Langley held out a small trinket box to Angel.

Surprised, Angel accepted it and opened it to find a beautiful diamond cameo broach. "Oh, you shouldn't have; you really shouldn't have. This is just too much," she said, still trying to get over the thought that Langley would ever think of anyone but himself. Anything from Langley would be more than she wanted. Angel winced. She knew that God would have to forgive her for that last thought. She tried to hand it back.

"You keep it," he said, curling his fingers around her hand and the broach and gently pushing it towards her. "Promise me that every time you look at it, you'll think of me, because I'll certainly be thinking of you. That's all the gift requires. Good day, Miss Angel." Langley gave a brief bow, then turned and left.

Angel watched him as he walked out, and for some reason she felt sorry for him. He was a rich young man that appeared to have everything within his grasp, and yet his emptiness preceded him. She looked down at the gift he had given her; she would always remember him when she looked at the broach, but not the way he wanted her to, because it would always be in prayer.

Wes and Billy had stopped by to tell Hank of the work they had finished but stopped in the hall when they heard him talking. When Hank spoke of Angel leaving, Wes felt a twist in his stomach that he

8

couldn't quite describe. He thought that life around the ranch was going to be a lot duller with Angel gone. Three years–that's a long time. He was pleased for his boss's family, yet for some reason he was feeling a bit sad. He shrugged his shoulders; brushing off the sadness, he guessed that all goodbyes felt that way.

Chapter Three

Angel looked over the land through the stagecoach window. This was the first trip she had been allowed to take alone, and she was excited. Momma had set things up with Aunt Lorraine, so that while Angel attended college, she would stay with them.

She remembered that Aunt Lorraine and Uncle Jim were fun. Angel had always enjoyed Lyndee, the one and only daughter they had. She was always full of life and could find humor in even the strangest of situations. Angel couldn't have been more pleased when she heard she would be staying with them.

Angel wished Momma and Papa hadn't cried when she left. That made her question her decision for a moment; and it added to her own doubts, making it even more difficult for her to leave. Her brothers had roughed up her hair and patted her on the back. To them it seemed like an adventure. Casey was sad, of course, but she promised to write him; and that seemed to cheer him up a little.

As Angel climbed into the coach, she spotted Wes out of the corner of her eye. He was smiling; then he nodded and gave her a quick wave. Turning back to her family, she felt a familiar twinge in her heart. It happened whenever she saw her family as she prepared for her trip. She knew she would miss all of them. "I can do all things through Jesus Christ, my Lord," she whispered aloud to herself, not just for comfort, but for encouragement too; and it steadied her nerves.

She settled back against the hard seat and knew it was going to be a long ride. Since she was well-acquainted with Montana's scenery, she decided she would nap while traveling through Montana. The rest of the way to Massachusetts, though, she wanted to be awake to see every state, city and town. She wanted to see all the popular tourist sites and commit them to memory, mostly because she wanted to have plenty to say in her letters when she would write loved ones back home.

The first city she reached was Fargo, the largest city in North Dakota. There Angel gathered her trunk and transferred to a Northern

Pacific train. It would be her first train ride, but also her first time sleeping anywhere but home. Excited, she bit her lip in anticipation.

She settled herself in a corner seat by the window. The train whistled as the conductor yelled, "All aboard!" It lurched forward, pushing Angel tight against her seat. She looked around her small cabin; the few travelers she sat with didn't seem to notice the sounds or the movement of the large locomotive. She guessed by their behavior that they must be seasoned travelers. She pressed her face to the window, enthralled just like a small child. She scanned the panoramic view, her eyes wide with anticipation, and soaked up every detail. After the train began its journey, she looked around and noted that the other travelers had fallen asleep almost instantly, so Angel decided to utilize this moment and took the opportunity to write her first letter home.

Dear Momma & Papa (and Brothers),

I'm on the train now and looking out the window at all the scenery. It's just beautiful! The wheat is flowering and so is the blue flax. They sway in the wind, and it looks like a field of little girls with long flowing blond hair, all of them moving in a rhythmic way, as if to the tune of a song; it's so graceful and peaceful to watch. It leaves me with a feeling of serenity.

I'm sitting next to a large woman with a small boy. The man across from me is a traveling salesman. He has a trunk full of wonderful gadgets, the likes of which I've never seen. He talks a lot but is very entertaining. They're all sleeping now, and the boy has his head on my lap. I guess I've made a friend. He reminds me of little Zach. He would've liked this trip and how I would've loved to have brought him.

I'm looking out the window again, and we're now just passing the Missouri River shoreline. Finally, some trees to see. Nature seems to take on a personality here. The trees stand proudly on the shore like tall soldiers all dressed in green. Their majestic limbs and leaves casting shadows on the river, while they tower over God's creations. The beaches are rocky, and the water is a clear blue. The waves are slapping at the shore; then they crash against the rocks, leaving a white foamy halo. I think the waves leave the shore a bit sad. They visit briefly and then splash and turn to make their way back out to the deep waters.

It's raining again. I think the sky was clear maybe just one day this week. I know it's our rainy season there; and my prayer is that all of you, along with the livestock and the fields, will make it through alright.

The rain is slapping against the windows again and making the sound of constant pitter-patter on the roof. I guess the rain has done its job and lulled me to sleepy land, so I'm going to close now. Please take care and may God Bless!

Love always, your Angel!

Angel quietly nestled her head on her little bag that she had placed behind her head. She didn't want to disturb the small boy and cause him to wake up. The song of the rains hitting the window, the chug-chug sound from the train's engine and the clanking from the wheels rolling on the tracks were all lulling her off to sleep. She petted the boy's head and hummed quietly. She was more tired than she was aware of, she quickly fell asleep and was gently rocked to a deeper rest by the train and by the small warm head in her lap.

*****

A tall young man peeked in the cabin and spotting Angel and the fellow passengers fast asleep. He quietly made his way over to Angel, then leaned down and whispered, "You're going to sleep the day away."

Angel opened her eyes with a start, "Excuse me...me?" she stuttered, trying to gather her wits about her. "Do I know you, sir?" she asked, rubbing her eyes.

The young man smiled congenially. "No, but let me introduce myself; I'm Matt," he said, extending his hand. "I noticed that you were traveling alone and thought you might want some company."

Somewhat flustered, she shook his hand then answered, "Well, at the moment," she whispered, "there doesn't seem to be more room for another person to sit next to me."

"I'll tell you what," he whispered back, "lunch is being served in the dining car, there's plenty of seating, and I would love to escort you."

"Oh, it's that late already? I am hungry." *Strangers are only friends you haven't met yet*, she thought for a moment while she assessed him. Grandma had told her that once, and besides, she had seen him around the station; and he seemed like a nice man. Angel smiled, "I'm flattered you find me a suitable luncheon guest. If you don't mind me tagging along, I'd love to join you. First, though, let me put this little boy on his mother. I don't think he's done sleeping." Angel smiled and gently lifted the boy's head; he muttered something about Mama, then curled under his mother's girth and went back to sleep.

Angel then held out her hand to Matt, and he quickly took it. Arriving in the dining car, they seated themselves at the table nearest the door.

"If you don't mind, I'll take the liberty to order for both of us," Matt offered.

"That would be just fine with me," Angel said, relieved. She had never had the opportunity to order her own food before, and she was feeling a bit awkward and also felt shy about it. The waiter approached, addressed them and took their order.

Matt closed the menu, "We'll have the soup and chicken sandwich special. Thank you." He handed the waiter their menus, then looking over at Angel, his face brightened. He cleared his throat, "So where are you headed?"

"Boston. I have family there," Angel answered.

"I've got family all over, but that doesn't mean I want to go visit them. Are you just visiting?"

"I am in a way. I'm going to stay with them while I attend college." She sat back to allow the waiter room to do his duties. He had brought tea and water and placed it before them.

Matt continued the conversation. "College," he mused aloud. "Well, that's quite an undertaking for a young woman. Do you have a major?"

"Teaching, I've always wanted to be one, and there is a need for teachers in our growing town." Angel, being interrupted, set her

13

napkin in her lap while the waiter set their dishes in front of them. Looking over the food, Angel's eyes grew big; and she realized she was hungrier than she had previously thought.

Matt laughed when Angel's eyes got bigger. "Help yourself; I'm sure we can order more food if the need arises."

"Oh, I'm sorry. It's just I haven't eaten since early morning, and I guess I'm quite hungry. I'm sure what we have here is more than sufficient; thank you." With that, the young duo dug into their food.

Matt continued their conversation, "Teaching is a demanding occupation, but fulfilling I hear. Have you any experience?"

Angel dabbed at the corner of her mouth, and then set her napkin in her lap. "It is demanding, but necessary. I have had a little experience." Then, feeling as if she were gushing but couldn't help it, she continued, "I helped teach Benjamin and Hannah to read this past summer. They don't attend school; they don't have much money, and their papa needs them on his farm to help with the chores. So, with permission, I took a few of my books over to their house; and when they would take time out for lunch, Mr. Montague allowed me to teach them. By the end of the summer, they could read and write. They even helped gather and count the chicken eggs for the market. Mr. Montague was happy about it and even thanked me. It was exciting and, I must agree with your earlier comment, very fulfilling." Angel smiled as she related her story to this attentive stranger.

"My, that's quite a story. Does your family agree with your decision to be a teacher?"

"Oh yes. In fact, they were the ones that paid for my education and this trip I'm on. I apologize for carrying on so. You must forgive me; it's just that I get excited when it comes to teaching. Well, enough about me. What is it that you do, and what brought you on this journey, Matt?" Angel asked with curiosity.

Matt smiled, "Oh, I travel quite a bit. I'm always looking for bargains and good deals; the better the deal, the bigger the profit. I sell pottery and such to the trading posts out west. I do alright for myself. However, I would like to find a place to call home, settle down with a nice girl. Sometimes it does get lonely." They finished their meal.

Matt pointed out landmarks they passed by and continued talking about his many trips and purchases. Angel wrapped half of her sandwich to take back to the boy in her compartment. Smiling as she remembered that little boys always have large appetites.

The following week Angel watched in awe as Matt pointed out the Ozark Mountains as they slowly traveled through them. Peering out her window, Angel put her finger on the glass and breathlessly exclaimed, "They're so beautiful. My goodness! One would think if you wanted to see God, all you had to do was stand at the top of one of those mountains. They look like they're as close to heaven as one can get."

"Yep, close enough for God to reach out and shake your hand." Gently covering her hand, Matt smiled in agreement.

Angel blushed and withdrew from his grasp. Sitting back in her seat, she tilted her head in approval of Matt's boyishly handsome good looks. By the look in his eyes, he seemed to know what Angel was thinking; and he too blushed.

Later sitting in her car, she reflected upon her day. Angel was glad she had accepted Matt's invitation; she had enjoyed their conversation and hoped secretly that they would spend more time together. "Of course, just to make the trip more enjoyable," she said, trying to convince herself. Angel laughed, "I think I can talk myself into anything."

When he held her hand, it brought back a few fleeting memories of a young man she couldn't really call a friend, but could consider a friendly acquaintance: Langley Williams.

With his father's insistence, he too traveled about, doing deals for land and treasures only he could afford. She ran into him on the streets in town many times in-between his travels. One in particular she remembered.

"Morning, Miss Angel." Langley had stopped in front of her, smiling and tipping his hat. "Are you coming or going?"

Angel fussed with her bonnet. Langley wasn't much of a charmer, but his good looks could ruffle a few feathers. "I'm going into the mercantile. Mama sent me with a list for material so we could make some dresses for school. And you, Langley, are you coming or going?"

15

Edith Gleason

"Well, I was going; but since I ran into you, I might stay a little longer." Angel's coin purse started to slip, and he reached out to recover it for her. She reached out; and as he placed it in her palm, he covered her hand in a soft squeeze.

Angel blushed. She was never one to turn down attention, but this felt a little uncomfortable. Clutching her purse, she gently pulled back her hand. Dejection showed in his eyes, and Angel felt sure he had never experienced that before.

"I thought maybe if you hadn't had lunch, you could accompany me to the hotel and get something to eat."

"I'd like that, but maybe some other time. Tim is in a hurry to get back to the ranch, and he gave me implicit orders to put a rush on it. Besides, Mama prepared a lunch basket for us. If you're going, then maybe you could join us on our way home," Angel offered.

"I'll have to reluctantly decline, Miss Angel. I remembered some other tasks that I need to attend to. You have a nice ride home." Langley tipped his hat again and walked over to the hotel.

On her trips to town she had spotted Langley numerous times watching her from across the street and always with a young lady on his arm, but he never attempted to approach her again.

The day she had boarded the stagecoach he had ridden his horse up to her window. "Miss Angel, I wanted to let you know I'll miss your sweet presence here. If I get to Boston, I wonder if it'd be alright if I looked you up."

Angel remembered being surprised that he even gave her a second thought, especially with all the young women he surrounded himself with. Being polite, she answered, "Yes that would be fine. My mother can give you the address that I'll be staying at."

"Wonderful. You take care of yourself, and I'll make it a point to look you up. Have a safe trip. Good day, Miss Angel." Langley half-smiled and rode away. Angel remembered being in awe as she smiled and waved to her family. She dropped her head and breathed a silent prayer for Langley.

"Father in Heaven, you know this man, Langley Williams. I know that he is lonely and that he needs you in his life. Help him and guide him to make that decision, so that he can be a better man and

16

no longer lonely. Amen."
After dinner one day, Angel took time away from her friend and pulled out her writing utensils from her satchel and penned another letter, this time to Casey.

Dear Casey,
I miss your humor and your company. I think this is the longest time we've ever spent away from one another. I've always thanked God for your friendship. I pray for you every day and am entertained by memories of your nonsensical adventures. I thank you for taking me along, and I hope you enjoy my journey with me through my letters.

The scenery that I have seen on my way is just wonderful. I wish you could see it. You would love it. I looked out today and spotted a single yellow flower on the side of a mountain. No one could've planted it there except God. It seems he's always pointing out the beauty of his creations.

It's amazing for me to think that something as tiny as a seed can become a flower, a tree, or a human being. God's creation knows just how tall or how small it should grow. He knows what color it should be and what it should look like. That's amazing!

It is such a blessing to think that God knows my name and that he knew me in the womb and knew I wanted to be a teacher. A scripture that comes to mind for me is, "He that started a good work in me will finish it..."

I'm sorry; I guess it must sound like I'm preaching. It's just that I'm overwhelmed by what God has done in nature and in my life.

By the way, I've made a new friend. His name is Matt; he's been making my journey a lot more interesting.

Well, back to home news. Have you been to the races? Has Wes been there, and did he win any of them? I hope so. You take care and please know I pray for you daily.

Love always,
Your friend, (I miss you)
Angel

Chapter Four

The train stopped in Milwaukee. From there Angel would take a coach, board a steam wheeler ferry in Saugatuck, then cross over Lake Michigan to arrive at the green shores of Michigan. Matt helped Angel with her trunk. Walking her over to the Inn, he bid her farewell.

"I'm certainly going to miss your stories and, of course, your company. I think I'm going to take the wagon train from here. You have a good trip and hopefully one day soon, I will see you again." With that, Matt leaned over and kissed Angel softly on the cheek.

"I'd hoped that we'd be traveling the whole distance together. I'm sorry to learn that's not the case. I'll miss your company as well. It's been a pleasure." Angel touched her cheek where he had kissed her and still felt the warmth from his lips. She tried to control her slight trembling as she held out her arm.

He squeezed her hand gently. "The pleasure was all mine, Miss Angel." Bowing faintly and tipping his hat, Matt stepped away and waved goodbye.

*****

Angel and the travelers booked the night in the town's Stagecoach Inn. An hour after they arrived, the weary travelers sat down to a hearty dinner. The heavy meal they ate would pretty much guarantee a good night's sleep for the exhausted passengers, and tonight Angel was one of them.

The chicken dinner with its gravy, mashed potatoes and biscuits were good; but nothing could compare to Momma's cooking. Already Angel missed her home and family. Later on in her small but adequate room, with a heavy sigh she sat on the edge of the bed, kneeled and offered up her evening prayers.

"Precious, heavenly Father," she began, "you know the very word on my tongue and every one of my thoughts. You know that I'm lonely and miss my home so very much. Thank you for your word. I will have trouble; but because of my belief in you, I will also be comforted. Please, Father, I ask for that comfort now. I know that this

18

journey will end, but give me what I need to make it through to the next promised glory. In Jesus' name I ask it all, Amen." Angel wiped her eyes. She felt comforted and was assured once more through prayer that she would make it alright.

Another scripture came to mind as she rose from her knees, "I can do all things through Christ that strengthens me." Angel smiled, then whispered, "Thank you, Lord." She was tired from the long bumpy ride on the train, yet somehow restless. She looked around the room; she didn't feel like writing, so she decided to go for a walk. Sitting on the edge of her bed, she put her boots back on and laced them up. It was getting closer to fall, which would explain the sudden chill she was experiencing, so she wrapped her shawl around her shoulders.

With a second thought occurring to her, she reached down and picked up her parasol. *It looked pretty cloudy when we came in, so maybe just in case it starts to rain.* Once she finished dressing, she made her way down the stairs and stepped out into the cool, humid night air.

"It's a fine night for a walk, Miss Angel; but one should never go unescorted. Would you like some company?"

Angel was surprised when she looked up to see Matt, the young man with whom she had spent most of her time on the train and had even shared her morning breakfast with. She had enjoyed their time together. *I guess God hears secret desires too.*

Tearing herself from her thoughts, she quickly answered, "Matt, I didn't know you were here! I thought you were going to ride along with the wagon train the rest of the way."

"Well, that was my plan, but the train doesn't depart until morning, so how about that walk? It's not good for a young lady to go unescorted. I hear I make a fine escort." He smiled.

"Yes, from my previous experience I'm sure you do. Please, by all means, join me." Matt stepped up next to her and offered his arm. "Matt, I know it was selfish of me to go on about myself and never ask where it is that you're headed. Is it too late if I ask you now?"

"Too late is only appropriate for the deceased. You weren't rude or selfish during our conversations. Actually I found you quite

19

charming, and I still do. The answer to your question is that my main destination is Boston, but I always wanted to see the sights along the way. I wanted to stop by a few more outposts and see what I could find, then make my way to where you're going. I thought I might try setting up a shop and staying in one place."

Matt stopped. "It looks like it's going to rain," he said, looking up at the dark clouds that had gathered. "Where are you going on your walk?"

"I wanted to stroll along the shoreline. That's something I never get to see in Montana. We don't have much shoreline; there presently isn't much water there. I've been writing my friend Casey, and I wanted to detail all of the scenery I've witnessed, so it would be like taking him on the trip with me. He could enjoy it as much as I do. I'm positively sure he would like the waters," Angel said as they strode along.

"Casey? That's a new mention. Is he a friend or maybe a boyfriend I should be worried about?" Trying to keep up with Matt's long strides, Angel picked up her steps.

"Oh no, it's not like that at all; we grew up together. His father is a hand on my Papa's ranch. Casey was born on our ranch a year before I was. I guess you could say we're best friends." She smiled in reminiscence of all their time together.

"Best friends. That's a good thing, since you're taking time out to share everything in writing with him. While we walk, how about sharing some things about Casey with me."

"Oh, I definitely have a lot of stories about Casey. He was always hatching up ideas, and he's always included me in everything. Albeit some things I would've rather he had not included me in."

"Are you telling me he's mischievous? Really, it sounds as if those stories could be entertaining. Please share them with me."

"No, that's okay; I don't want to be a bother."

"Would I have asked if I thought it would bother me? Let me answer that… no. Please, go ahead." He grinned.

"Well, alright, since you insist; but you must promise me you won't think badly of Casey. He's mischievous, but his heart is in the right place."

20

"I promise I won't think badly of Casey." Angel smiled; she was amazed how comfortable Matt could make her feel. He made it easy for her to talk to him.

"Well, the first one I remember happened when we were in school. He sat behind a girl named Crystal. Every day he would wait until we would get out our chalkboards, and she had to erase something. Then he would dip her long, black braid, in the ink wells that were on their desks. He wanted to see how long it would take her to figure out how ink got in her hair. Well, after about three days, she looked at his desk and saw black string marks. She knew the girls that sat behind her were her friends. She also knew Casey could sometimes be a troublemaker. So she sat in her seat and waited to feel the tug on her hair. During our math lesson, she felt it. She turned around and punched Casey square in the face, leaving him with the biggest shiner I have ever seen; and I have four brothers."

"What did your teacher do?"

Angel giggled, "Miss Minchin did nothing. She said she figured it was enough punishment for him to have to explain where he got his shiner."

Matt laughed with her, "Is that all he did?"

"No, not even close. The most recent thing I remember was serving a couple of girls that we had some problems with some cow dung sandwiches."

Aghast, Matt asked, "Why would he do a thing like that?"

"It's kind of a long story. You sure you want to hear it?" she asked.

"How could I resist a story like that?"

Angel took a deep breath and continued, "These two girls, Rachel and Caitlyn, were always ruining my lunches. The last time they ruined it, they had put ants on my sandwich. Casey was more upset than I was. I had other things to eat, but he said that was it; it was time to get them back.

The next day he began to schmooze with them and let them think he was their best friend. After a week of that behavior, he brought a big sacked lunch. He proclaimed to the girls that he had brought enough lunch for them both, and he wanted them to join him at lunch.

21

They all agreed, so when it came time to eat, all of the girls sat under the apple tree; and he passed out the apples and sandwiches. Unbeknownst to them, he had put special ingredients on the sandwiches: cow dung. The cow dung was dried out when he put it on bread with mustard and butter. When it's dry, it doesn't smell as strong. Well, the girls kind of wrinkled their noses when they saw the food and looked at Casey. He gave them his biggest smile, then took a bite of his own unhampered sandwich. Well, the girls didn't want to offend their new friend, so they smiled back and took a big bite. You never saw such spitting and throwing up in your life. He got paddled and sent home for that one."

"It sounds to me as if he came to your rescue, Angel. Kind of a circumstance hero, I'd say."

Angel looked at the heavy, dark, moving clouds and thought for a moment. "Yes, I think you're right. He's always been there for me." Rain drops began to fall on the young couple and interrupted their conversation. Angel hurriedly put up her parasol and lifted her dress to keep it from getting wet and dragging in the soon-to-be mud.

"I think our walk is over. It's late and raining, so I'm going to head back to the inn. I hope my stories didn't bore you, and I hope to see you in Boston, Matt. It's always nice to have a friend, and then everyone you see is not a stranger. Goodnight." Angel tipped her head, and then, gathering more of her dress up into her hands, she ran to the shelter of the inn.

Matt stood in the rain for a few moments and smiled to himself. He watched her as she hurried inside. "Indeed, it's always nice to have a friend," he said aloud with a sneer; then, turning around, he headed toward the tavern, which is where he was to meet up with his partner Joshua.

The two men had been plotting their kidnapping scheme since they had been to Canada, where they had attended the cattle round up and sale. That's where they ran into Angel's father, Mr. Hank Winters. They became curious after they watched as Hank pulled a large role of bills out of his breast pocket and paid for his purchase of twenty head of cattle.

"Did you see that, Matt? That's the biggest wad of money I've ever seen," Joshua asked his friend.

"I saw it. I've never seen more. I think we need to figure out a way to part Mr. Winters from his money," Matt said. That's when the notion of greed crawled up inside of the men and caused them to inquire about Hank from the other ranchers.

After that, the men followed and watched Hank closely and yet went unnoticed by the other busy men. Later in the dark recesses of the tavern, they discussed their findings.

"Everywhere he goes his men are right beside him," Joshua explained. "There's no way we can take on that many men and survive."

"Isn't that what living is all about? Which chances to take and which ones you'll survive?' Matt asked sarcastically.

"Matt, is money worth dying for?" Joshua pleaded.

"Obviously not our money, but the Winters' cash might be worth it."

"Ba, ha, ha, ha, you are too funny. Yep, we ain't got a dime, but we will soon!" Joshua bellowed.

"And lots of 'em," Matt added; and then both men clanked their glasses of whiskey in agreement and gulped down their beverages.

Joshua swiped at his mouth with the back of his hand, "How we gonna do that, Matt? You got plans?"

"Of course, we'll follow him back to Butte and see how we can accomplish this task." Matt finished, and then ordered another drink. "Yep, they won't even know we're coming. Like a thief in the night, my friend. Like a thief in the night."

Lying low and careful not to draw attention to themselves, Joshua and Matt set up their camp on a nearby mountain. They set up their spy glass to make sure they could keep a close watch of the ranch and the people within. They went for food and water at night and slept without a campfire. Not wanting to draw attention with smoke from the fire, they ate cold beans and bread.

"Look at that. They got one daughter, and it looks like they dote on her," Joshua noted on the third day.

"From what I know about the nature of man, every man has a weak spot, and I think we found Mr. Winters'. When we were in

Edith Gleason

town last night, I overheard a few of the cowboys saying that the Winters' girl was real sweet; and they were going to miss her when she went to Boston," Matt related.

"Sounds like them cowboys know her real good like," Joshua remarked.

"Yep, one named Wes. I don't remember the other one's name, but from what I gathered, they both do some work for the Winters. I trust its good information, and we're going to go with that. Ya feel like taking a trip to Boston?" Matt asked his anxious friend.

"You bet. Just tell me when."

"When," Matt answered. That was months ago; and with a lot of planning, Matt and Joshua set their plan into action. Matt shook his head to help clear his thoughts.

"So this trip the family has sent her on," he murmured to no one out loud, "will make her more vulnerable than they know. Boston is a big city; and people can get lost there, especially young, unescorted females." Yes, she was worth something to the Winters' family; and, if things went according to plan, it looked like receiving a ransom was going to be a sure bet for the two scheming men.

24

Chapter Five

Angel looked around for Matt. "I just want to say goodbye. And maybe see him one last time," she told herself. But after an exhaustive search, she couldn't locate him. She had inquired of the innkeeper but had no luck. Walking disappointedly to the boat, she cheered herself with one remaining thought; *I'll probably see him again. After all, we're heading in the same direction.* It was nothing she knew, just something she felt.

Lake Michigan was beautiful. The steam wheeler ferry was steady amongst the huge waves that pushed it along as they sometimes crashed at its side. The ferry rocked and leaped and chugged along, holding its passengers in tow.

Angel looked over the side of the ferry. She seemed to look down forever, deep into the water. It was a clear blue with the reflection of the sky, making it appear endless. She could understand why sailors chose life on the sea, with its pitches of ups and downs, yet with its calming rocking that could lull a baby to sleep. She thought of how Jesus had fallen asleep in a boat.

The shore of Michigan arrived too soon for Angel. She stepped out onto a sandy beach with tall pine and maple trees towering over the water, casting huge shadows with their branches that seemed to reach out and pull you onto the shore. She and her fellow passengers hopped aboard a wagon that would transport them to the train. Once on board Angel seated herself but couldn't take her eyes away from the window.

"It's beautiful, isn't it?" spoke a plump, pleasant-looking woman seated across from her.

Angel sat back, exclaiming in agreement, "Yes, it is beautiful. I've never seen so much water with lush grassy hills for a backdrop. It's a perfect picture. I want to soak it up and hope I never forget it."

"You won't. Anything that makes that big of an impression stays with us. You go ahead and enjoy it, dear. This is my third trip out this way, so I'm going to settle back and take a short nap." Closing her eyes and leaning her head back, she quickly opened her eyes

25

again and offered, "Oh, by the way, my name is Jessica. Please feel free to call me Jessie. By the way, it's no mistake that you're in my car. I met your father on one of my trips. He told me of your desire to attend college to be a teacher. I could tell he was proud of you. I saw it in his eyes. He asked me if I would accompany you for part of your long journey. Of course I was bit hesitant at first, but I'm glad I conceded. You seem like a very pleasant young woman with a good head on her shoulders. I hope you find me as pleasant a companion."

Angel thought to herself, it was just like papa to take care of her, even from a distance. She extended her hand in greeting, "I'm Angel Winters and I'm pleased to meet you, Ma'am."

"Likewise, Angel, and the pleasure is all mine." Miss Jessie shook her hand in greeting, "Oh, look at forgetful me. I forgot to take care of my things. I guess I should do that before I go to sleep. That sounds like the right order. How about that, Angel? Does that sound right to you?" Miss Jessie winked and smiled. Angel nodded in agreement.

Cumbrously the woman stood; and reaching up, she placed her luggage in the overhead compartment. Sitting down on her seat with a plop, she exhaled loudly, "If I'm still sleeping when lunch arrives, would you be a dear and please wake me up? I didn't get to be this pleasingly plump by missing too many meals," she said, patting her stomach.

"Yes, Miss Jessie," said Angel, smiling at her reference, "I'll be sure to wake you when it comes."

"Thank you, Angel. Now if you don't mind." Jessie laid her head back on her seat and quickly nodded off. Angel found it amusing at how her snoring was in unison with the sounds of the chugs from the train. That seemed to make Miss Jessie even more endearing. Angel's eyes took her back to the views scrolling past her window. It was all so breathtaking; she didn't want to miss a second of it.

Traveling through Michigan was quick. Angel hardly noticed the difference in scenery when they passed through Ohio with their green forests and great waters; both places left a forever impression on Angel.

Marietta, Ohio, had been the first settlement in America, and it was huge and full of people. Angel enjoyed looking out the window and seeing the diversity of the busy citizens. Watching until all the scenery and people were out of sight, Angel sighed; it had passed by too soon, and she settled back to await her arrival in New York.

The train whistle woke Angel with a start. For some reason she had forgotten she was on a train. She was dreaming of home and could still hear Casey's laughter. But during their friendly cavorting, a small curly-headed boy warned, "Watch out for the shadows, Ainjo." Then giggling, he ran ahead. Angel recognized the chubby hands of her brother Zach. Sometimes he called her Ainjo because he had trouble with the pronunciation. "Baby, you're always in my dreams," she whispered and so wanted to give in to the small cry welling up inside her; but she was interrupted by the gentle voice of a female friend who cajoled her awake.

"Come, dear, New York City is one of the largest cities in America. This is where we will spend the night. There is an inn here called Stamford House. We'll send our bags over and settle in later. Right now let's hurry and look around, Angel; there is so much to see." Jessie noticed Angel's hesitation, then added, "It will give you more to write home about."

Angel, wiping her eyes, sat up and looked about. It was a huge city and a little bit frightening to the western small-town girl, "I don't know if I should. I don't want to get lost."

"You won't, dear; we'll look together." Not being able to contain her excitement for her new friend any longer, Miss Jessie pulled Angel's hand. Angel was up quickly on her feet and without objection; she was surprised that any woman could have that much strength in their grasp. Miss Jessie gave another pull; and with a whoosh, Angel's hesitation was gone, and they were off. Both women were blissfully unaware of the two shadowy figures that followed closely behind them and watched their every move.

The shops were amazing and Angel looked around in awe. She had never seen so many different shops in one place. There were tobacco, grocery shops, butcher shops, millinery, shoe stores, drug stores, furnishings, dry goods, banks and even candy shops. That was the place Miss Jessie liked the most. She said one day she would open her own candy store.

For right now she would enjoy the delicacies someone else made and figure out some recipes later. Of course, Angel bought a little bit of taffy for herself too. Father had put her on a spending budget, but it was only one small indulgence she felt she could afford. After tasting it, she knew it had been money well-spent.

New York Central Park was more than she thought it would be. There were statues and flowers of every color lining the walks. There were street vendors and live music with Shakespearean actors performing plays on makeshift stages. Overheated ladies sat on benches beneath their parasols, fanning themselves while waiting for the men to finish their game of horseshoes.

Children of every size ran and frolicked with one another playing chase and picking flowers, all of them oblivious to what their parents were doing. There were men in three-piece suits discussing the day's politics and business. They wore watches on chains hanging from their vest pockets and tall black hats which sat squarely on their heads.

Angel giggled when she noticed that with every nod, the men's hats tilted in unison with their conversations, yet never once fell. The park was full of life, and Angel loved it.

It was getting late, so Miss Jessie and Angel walked back to the inn and checked into their rooms. After receiving their keys, they walked around past the many rooms. They walked past the gentlemen's smoking room, past the parlor and the dining room where people were just finishing their dinner.

The inn was decorated so ornately, the wood flooring shone like the noonday sun in all its glory. Velvet red drapes hung from the top of the windows down to the floors and were tied off in the middle with gold ropes. The sheer beauty of the place took Angel's breath away.

After visiting all of the shops in the downstairs, they noticed that time had passed quickly; it was time for dinner and they were hungry. Miss Jessie and Angel both made their way back up the carpeted stairs where they were escorted to a table by a distinguished-looking gentleman. The famished women sat down to a quiet meal but still not without two unscrupulous men watching each bite of food the women ate.

"I've never seen so much beauty in one place!" Angel exclaimed.

"Oh, this is nothing compared to the inns in Boston. I'm positive you'll be impressed with my hometown. I am and I've lived there all of my life." Miss Jessie dabbed at her chin with her napkin. "Do you want this last piece of bread before I take it? I wouldn't want to waste away to nothing," she joked. "I think my appetite has grown since we've been here. Probably from all that walking we did today; I'm sure that's it," Miss Jessie finished, having answered her own question.

Angel smiled to herself. She liked Miss Jessie and was glad they had become such fast friends. If Miss Jessie wanted to answer her own question, that was just fine with Angel.

After dinner, the ladies made their way to their rooms where they quickly gave into the filling food and wave of exhaustion from their trip; a bed would feel good to both of their generations.

Morning came, and her adventure ended too soon when she heard the conductor calling, "All aboard!" Angel and Miss Jessie, each holding packages of newly-acquired treasures, hopped on the train and once again settled into their seats.

"Next stop, Boston, Massachusetts!" the porter called. Angel held her breath; she had finally arrived at her destination.

Chapter Six

It was raining in Boston. The sky was full of black, billowy clouds that cast a noonday shadow over the damp city. The clock tower rang out the bongs of 2:00. Taking her hand, the conductor helped Angel step down from the train. With the same help, Miss Jessie was right behind her.

"If you don't have anyone meeting you here, dear, you're welcome to ride in my carriage; and I'll take you to your aunt's house," Miss Jessie offered.

"My aunt and uncle said they would be here around 4:00. I think they'd be awfully disappointed if they came and I wasn't here. I truly don't mind waiting for them. I'll just spend some time getting to know the city and look around in the shops. I won't wander too far. Thank you for the offer. I have your address and I will be looking you up. I'd love for you to meet my family," Angel said, politely declining her offer.

"Well, fine then if you're comfortable doing that; I've got your address too, so I will be looking you up as well. I've got to see how you're getting along. I feel I've found a new friend. Miss Angel, it's been a pleasure." Miss Jessie gave a quick curtsy to Angel and then stepped up into her carriage. Once inside she leaned out the window, smiled and waved goodbye to her new friend.

Angel had her large trunk deposited at the train depot, leaving only her small handbag which she carried with her. Walking and looking around at the tall, round, red-bricked buildings, she spotted a dress shop and decided she would go in; it would help give her an idea what the local townspeople were wearing.

The women inside were very accommodating and friendly as they showed her the latest styles. Angel knew that she would never be able to afford them, especially on a student's salary; but it gave her some ideas for dresses she would make for herself later.

Angel thanked the ladies and left to get acquainted with the rest of the city. She peered into the shop windows and sometimes wandered inside. She was still unaware of the two stealthy shadowy figures that followed her every move.

She stepped off the sidewalk and crossed the street to watch the street performers with their monkeys. She watched as they would dance to the musical box songs; she clapped and laughed along with the crowd. Her only regret was that she didn't have a penny to drop in the hat the man passed around when he was finished.

Afterward, she stopped in the park and listened to the Shakespearian players and walked away feeling somewhat confused by the language. Angel pieced off a small chunk of bread from her half sandwich she had saved from the train and fed the small flock of birds that were squawking as they gathered at a statue nearby.

That had been the last of her food rations, and she was feeling hunger pains. She decided to go buy a sausage from the street vendor and sat on a park bench to eat her lunch. She observed the people while she ate and found that one could be easily entertained just by observing the people going about their business in this big city. Angel came to the conclusion that Boston was an interesting place, and she would enjoy everything about Boston while she was here.

It was early fall, so darkness came at an earlier time. When she saw the daylight slowly giving way to darkness, Angel took note of the time. She quickly picked up her pace and headed back to the station; she didn't want to lose her way and get lost in the streets of a strange city. Hurrying along, Angel was so enthralled by the city's activities that she hadn't given thought to watch where she was going until she ran smack dab into a tall man's chest.

"What a surprise to meet you again and so soon. Where are your companions? I thought you were meeting your aunt and uncle here." Matt stood in front of Angel, placing his hands on her shoulders.

"Matt!" Angel replied with a start. "It is a surprise. I'm sorry. I've got to start paying better attention, at least to where I'm going. I'm on my way now to meet them. That's why I'm hurrying." Looking down at her watch, she knew that her aunt and uncle would be here soon to pick her up and that she didn't have time to dawdle, so she tried to politely excuse herself.

"I'm glad to see you again, although I didn't think it would be this soon; but I need to get back to the station. If I'm not there, my

31

aunt and uncle will start to look for me. I wouldn't want to cause them any grief."

"Well, we can't have that, can we?" Matt tipped his hat and stepped out of Angel's way. "I hope to see you again, Miss Angel, and soon."

Angel thought that was a forward thing to say, when really she hardly knew him. She looked back at him and thought she saw him sneering, but she dismissed it and nodded in her haste, "Yes, soon," she replied and hurried off, unaware that the two dark figures still followed close behind her.

Walking briskly past a couple of small businesses that had closed for the day, she came upon an alley. A small voice whispered in Angel's ear, "Herwy, Ainjo, don't go down there." Angel stopped for a moment and quickly looked around. She watched to see the little person that could whisper so close to her ears. Because of the hour, the streets were somewhat deserted and she saw no one in sight. "Zach," she murmured, then touched her ear; a feeling of gratefulness overcame her as she accepted that even in the hereafter he would watch over her. Why he would care about her at all was beyond her.

Recently she had accepted that it was his soft voice that would speak to her at odd hours and in some way always a help. She shook her head. She couldn't think about that right now; she was in a hurry. Besides, there was no one in sight. Careful not to drag her skirts in the mud, she lifted them and stepped down off the walk.

Angel didn't see the set of strong arms that jerked her off her feet and into the alley passage. Another set of strong arms that were waiting roughly and quickly took hold of her while trying to tie her hands and secure her mouth with a gag.

Angel tried to scream and kick at her assailants, but she was no match for the strong men. As she was wriggling and trying to scream for help, an unknown fist flew into the air and connected with one of the men's jaws that sent him flying against the wall. As Angel watched him slide to the ground, another fist slammed into the other man's stomach, causing him to double over and gasp for air as he crumpled to the ground. Released suddenly from both of the men's

32

grasps, Angel tumbled to the ground. She watched in fear and confusion at the commotion that was taking place in front of her.

Another uniformed man seemed to come out of nowhere and entered into the small ring of turmoil. After much thrashing and grunting, the two men were wrestled down to the ground. Then in what seemed like an eternity to Angel but was actually only a few moments, the two men who had tried to accost her lay motionless on the muddied ground. Pulling herself up, she stood back against the wall and looked up into her Uncle Jim's face, friendly and jolly as always, but reddened from the exertion.

"I've always loved a tussle. I hope these two men weren't your friends," he teased. Looking the ruffians over, he answered, "I think not. Let's call the law and have these two hoodlums locked up where they belong," Uncle Jim said, pleased with himself and holding both men by the scruffs of their necks.

"No need to, sir; here in this part of town I am the law. I hern the tussle out on the street and I came to investigate. I can take it from hern, sir. I've got me a pepperbox and Paddy whacker if'n dey git out a line. I won't be hornswaggled by the likes of these piddlin knucks." The young Irish officer looked over at Angel, "Are ye all right, wee lass?"

"I am now, thanks to my uncle and you."

"Twas nothing, just doin me job. Let me take these two knucks off yourn hands and let yourn kind people go bout yourn business." The officer grabbed the two men. "They'll 'ave time ta think 'bout what they done when they be layin' in jail tonight."

"And your name is?" asked Uncle Jim.

"Aye, ye be wantin' me name. Tis Officer Patty or Patrick McGee ye be callin' me, at yourn service," he said, bowing and smiling at Angel.

"You stop by my place, young man; and my wife will whip you up something delicious for dinner in return for your help here tonight. Here's my address. Just stop by any time this week. It'll be my pleasure this time to serve you."

"Aye, I will, evening." With that he led the criminals to their destiny.

33

Edith Gleason

Uncle Jim turned to Angel, "You look just like your momma, Angel. I'd have recognized you anywhere. You're not hurt, are you?" he asked as he looked her over for injuries. "Naw, just a little dirt," he answered himself, "and maybe your pride. I hear that always goes before a fall." Angel smiled as she brushed herself off.

Uncle Jim continued, "I hope you have a good time here while you're with us. I'm still awful sorry about the welcome you received. We'll see if we can make it up to you somehow," he promised. Together they watched as another lawman joined Patrick and helped escort Matt, a man she thought was her friend, and his partner Josh off to jail.

Uncle Jim lifted her bag and put his big arm around her shoulder. He then pulled her close in a gentle hug saying, "You'll be alright now; Jesus retrieved our lamb. Hey, Precious," And as if the thought just occurred to him, he stated, "Let's go see your new home and while we're at it, reclaim your trunk on the way."

Angel, just barely getting her ground, smiled, "That would be great, Uncle Jim; please lead on."

Stepping down from her uncle's coach, her feet had barely touched the ground when Angel was swiftly lifted off her feet by her excited chubby cousin, Lyndee. Both her red curly hair and her skirt were flying. Lyndee gleefully grabbed up Angel and swung her about. Angel hung on for dear life but laughed and giggled along with her cousin.

At last Lyndee set her down and exclaimed, "It's been too long, little cousin; and we got a lot of catching up to do. Come on, I'll show you your room. We're going to have a lot of fun while you're here; and, if we can't find any, we'll make our own," Lyndee promised with a little more mischievous glee than was proper. Angel's reply was just a smile.

Chapter Seven

"You're kidding! Matt walked and talked with you and then tried to kidnap you?" Lyndee asked with disbelief.

"Yes," Uncle Jim infused. "The sheriff said that when he and his deputies were searching their hotel room, he found a ransom note and a map of your Uncle Hank's home. They weren't asking for a little money, either. Nasty pair, those two are. Thankfully, with the help of young Patty, we were able to put those no-do-gooders where they belong. You can bet Angel wouldn't have walked away from it either, not alive anyways. The good Lord had other plans."

"I'm really grateful to you, Uncle Jim. I shudder to think what could've happened. I hope that's as exciting as it gets here, because I think that's all I can handle." Angel was truly exhausted from her ordeal, not to mention a little sore from the tussle in the alley.

"Young Patty, huh, is he cute?" Lyndee looked over at Angel to see her yawning; she jumped up and took Angel's hand, "Come on with me. You can tell me all about your young rescuer tomorrow; I think you deserve a good night's rest. We'll talk more in the morning. We'll have time then; and, if we get up early enough, I'll show you around the place."

Angel smiled with relief, then stood and left with her cousin. At this point, sleep didn't sound too bad at all. She prayed Momma and Papa didn't get too upset when they received her aunt's telegram about the whole ordeal. She was so far away, and Momma always liked to comfort her with a hug. She thought that her family would be alright with what happened to her because, after all, she was safe; and that's what really mattered.

As soon as Angel's head hit her pillow, she closed her eyes; but sleep would not come. An uneasy feeling crept over her. She was sure it was fear, and it was a recent lesson from her torment in the alley.

Angel knew that there was no fear in perfect love and that perfect love casts away all fear. She thought about it and came to the conclusion that this kind of fear could make you more aware of your

35

surroundings; maybe it was a healthy fear.

She trusted the Lord and wanted to give this fear to him; but like so many other things in life, something inside her made her hold onto it. Angel opened her eyes and scanned the room; in the night anything could be scary with black and grey colors and the shadows they cast.

She reached over to her bedside table and, finding a match, lit her candle. Lifting her candle high, she looked around the room; she saw that everything was as it should be. Then she placed the candle back on the stand. Angel broke down into a prayer, "Please, God, don't let me fear what you have made."

She cried out in the night to her heavenly Father, "Instill in me the knowledge that you are God of the nights as well as the days. I don't want to be afraid, and I don't want to hold onto this man-made fear. Take it, Lord; I give it freely to you. Wrap me in your arms of love and grant me a peaceful sleep. I thank you, Father, for getting me through one more trial." Angel knew there would be many more trials in her life as she continued, "I entrust in you all of my tomorrows and my right now. I ask it all in Jesus' name, Amen."

A verse came quickly to Angel's thoughts, *"Preserve me, O God, for in thee do I put my trust."*

"Thank you, Father," she offered. Angel blew out the candle and laid her head on her pillow. As soon as her head hit her pillow this time, her eyes closed; and sleep came quickly and ended a most tiresome day.

*****

"Get up, little cousin." Lyndee was nudging Angel, trying to roust her from sleep. "Time's a wasting and there's so much to see."

"I'm awake; I'm awake! You can stop nudging me now." Angel rubbed her arm in the spot where Lyndee had been pushing.

"Well, all I see is that your eyes are still closed. And if you get up like that, you're going to be running into stuff." Lyndee put her hands on her hips, as if she were assessing the situation. She grabbed the covers and gave a yank which, of course, sent Angel tumbling to the floor, blankets and all.

"Lyndee, what do you think you are doing?" Angel sat up and

demanded, aghast.

"That's how we get things done here in Boston. Hurry up and get dressed, Angel; breakfast is waiting." Lyndee whirled around and hurried down the stairs; and Angel, who had already forgiven her, wasn't far behind her.

Breakfast had been good, but Angel missed Momma's pancakes. Angel missed everything from home. She wished her brothers were here with her now; that would calm her, but so much for wishful thinking. Tomorrow Uncle Jim would take her to sign up for her college courses. Her stomach was a little upset.

It made her nervous to think of going off to a place where she didn't know anyone, but she prayed the Lord would give her a good friend. She knew the Lord wouldn't let her down. Maybe it was the pancakes that made her stomach upset; after all, Lyndee made them. "I shouldn't think that. It wasn't very nice, but I'm sure she would forgive me," Angel told herself as she helped clean up.

Chapter Eight

Patrick's reasoning might have been selfish as he rode his mare up to the front steps of the brownstone house that Mr. Jim called his home. He was hesitant at first to accept his gracious invitation and even thought of declining it in the name of duty. He thought better of it, though, when he remembered Angel's sky-blue eyes and the most angelic smile he had ever seen. He accepted his reasoning and dismounted his horse. Then, after tying his horse to the post, he made his way up the steps and rapped softly on the front door.

He questioned himself again. *Maybe,* he thought, *I should have put a little distance in between last night and today; after all, I don't want to appear desperate.* But, like all good Irish boys, he remembered the words of his Ma', "The early bird gets the worm." When there was no response, he rapped a little louder on the door.

The door slowly opened as Lyndee's form filled the doorway. "Well, my, and you must be the young officer that came to my cousin's rescue," stated Lyndee, never being one to mince words.

Smiling and removing his cap, Patrick responded, "Aye, that I am. And are Mr. Jim and Miss Angel in?"

"Let the boy in, Lyndee. We can't leave our guest out on the front stoop," Uncle Jim called out as he approached Patrick. He then led him to the dining room, where Aunt Lorraine was serving up dinner for the family and now a hungry guest. "Sit down and don't be afraid to help yourself. There's plenty to go around," Uncle Jim offered.

"Now, Jim, don't overwhelm the boy; we just met, and we'll want him to come back." Aunt Lorraine beamed, "I hear you saved our little Angel from those no-do-gooders. I thank you not just for us, but for her parents too."

"It was nothing, Ma'am. I wouldn't be human if'n I didna want ta help," Patrick answered as he seated himself next to Angel.

"No, you were a Godsend, and we'll always thank the Lord for you. Papa, now that everyone is seated, how about you offer up the evening meal prayer so we can eat?"

The dinner guests bowed their heads. "Dear Lord, for the food we're about to eat, we thank you kindly. We ask that you bless it to our bodies. And for this young man you've put into our lives, we also thank you. We ask that you bless his life very well and those around him. In Jesus' name we ask it all, amen." Uncle Jim raised his head, "Let's eat. Pass the chicken, please."

Dinner had been good. Patrick liked the chicken and dumplings, and Angel's corn bread was to die for. After dinner, he sat with Angel in the parlor and talked for a long time.

"How long do ye plan on bein' here, Angel?"

"Until I finish school, as far as I know." Patrick listened intently to Angel and thought she was sweeter than the first time he had seen her. With a smile, he thought, *she looks prettier every time I glance at her*.

Angel liked the way Patrick looked, with his curly black hair that had a tussled appearance; and the green shirt he wore made his bright green eyes seem piercing. He was a boyish kind of pretty. He wasn't very tall, and so he jokingly blamed his stature on his uncles. "Aye, me uncles are tiny people; and me Ma, she's too good to blame anythin' on."

They talked and laughed with Uncle Jim way into the early morning hours. That's when Angel discovered that Patrick was also enrolled in college; he was a pre-med student. He said his uncle got him the job as a cop and that the money he made as a policeman was paying for his education. He would be finished with his schooling and go on to London to finish his studies just months before Angel would graduate.

Patty left in the quiet of the dawn. Angel bid him a good day. With a smile and a promise to escort her to school on Monday, he was off.

*****

Monday morning came, and Lyndee was the one rushing Angel around, "Come on, Angel. Papa has the coach waiting out front. Do you have your books and supplies?"

"Yes, Mother," Angel jokingly called her. "I gathered them last night. Lyndee, what am I going to do without you there to take care of me?"

39

Edith Gleason

"You'll do just fine, little cousin. Just pray and talk to the Lord. He'll give you all the confidence you need."

Angel knew that, but it didn't take away all her apprehension. She was putting on her wrap when a surprised Lyndee announced, "Well, I'll be, Officer Patty is here."

"Oh, that's right; he promised he would escort me. Tell him I'm coming." Angel was out the door before Lyndee could finish her sentence, causing all of them to laugh as Patty helped Angel up into the carriage. *It's funny,* Angel thought, *my apprehension seems to have disappeared.*

Chapter Nine

The classrooms were bigger than Angel thought they would be, and the long hallways seemed endless. The scholars carried themselves with significance. They discussed events and courses as they went rushing from class to class.

Angel liked her professors. One she liked in particular was Professor Jordan; he was Jewish. This was the first time she had ever met anyone from the Holy Land. He was so personable, and his lectures were taught *to* you, instead of *at* you.

Rushing from her math class to her English class, she ran head-on into Patty. Looking up, she was caught off-guard. His devious grin and the way Patrick looked at her caused her to blush.

"Going somewhere?" he asked. "Don't let me get in the way."

"Yes, and I'm surprised I didn't knock you off your feet!" she replied.

"It'd take a bigger person than ye ta do that. Will ye be ridin' home with me?" he inquired.

"Of course, that's what we planned. Plus I'm starving. Tomorrow I'll make a big lunch for us; and since you're so noble that you give me a ride, I'll supply our nutrition."

"We can sit in the dining room and enjoy each other's company, sounds like we 'ave a plan. Aye, I'll meet you out front." They both nodded in agreement and went about their ways.

Angel rushed to her class and sat down quickly. She didn't want to miss a word from her professor. She listened with rapt attention to Professor Jordan. He believed in what he said, and for her that made it so much more interesting. She loved to listen to storytelling, and he was good at it. History had never been her favorite subject; that is, until now.

Professor Jordan put his chalk down and addressed the class, "Our history, like most history, began with lawlessness. Gunslingers were prevalent at the beginning of our states and still are, even now as I speak. I remember reading a town docket about two men being involved in a showdown in the middle of town. One was shot down

41

Edith Gleason

instantly while the other was gut shot. You see the gunslinger's entrails and stomach parts lay in the slinger's own hands."

The professor explained as he folded his hands in front of his stomach, "The town doctor put his insides back in place but still couldn't save him. Both men were good shots because that's what they did for a living or had to do sometimes just to survive.

"So men had a chance of going down; it was a fifty-fifty chance, and gunmen seemed to thrive on that. I guess the only thing we could gather from their behavior is that shotguns and rifles are for hunting, and sidearms are for killing men."

After finishing his lecture, the professor gave the class an assignment to research: where gunslingers came from and why. He explained, "History isn't always about origins, but also about the fact that everything a person does becomes a part of their own personal history; and history is made every day. Class is dismissed."

After school, Angel greeted Patty out front where they had agreed to meet. He met her with a huge smile and then helped her up into the carriage. The ride home was exhilarating to Angel as Patty told her about his classes, and she in return reiterated the stories Professor Jordan had told.

"I can clearly relate to that because of places that I've been on my job." Patty relayed some of his stories but was careful to leave out any gruesome details. He said that it wasn't a suitable discussion for a lady.

Angel liked Patty because he was so easy to talk to. In their conversations he had told her, "It was a different way of life in me Ireland." He loved to talk about his homeland, and Angel loved to hear his stories.

"Ye will 'ave ta stop me if'n I go ta far, but I ne'er miss an opportunity to talk 'bout me homeland. The enchanted moors, they're filled with bogs and gloomy mists, make the imagination run a bit wild. Ah, and the countryside, it's 'ard for eryone to walk the rocky hill terrain, of course, lessen yourn a goat," he joked. "The weather is cold 'n rainy, but it only adds to the beauty o' the land."

Angel listened enraptured, "Do you miss Ireland, Patty?" she asked when he stopped for a breath.

After the Rains

"Aye, I miss it greatly, especially me buds. Me ma, I thinks she likes it 'ere."

"Do you have any other family members besides your mother and cousins?" Angel found Patty one of the most interesting people she had ever met and wanted to learn as much as she could about him.

"Aye, I 'ad a sister, Addie; but she died from the croup when she was but a babe. I was five when it came through our town, but I was stronger and fought it off. Me Da was lost at sea. He was a fisherman. Me ma was a maid for Mr. Webster. He was the town's prosecutor. He was more of a friend than a boss, though. I think 'e wanted ta marry me ma, but she would'n 'ave it. Said she wanted ta raise 'er son first, that bein' me."

Patty smiled and did a slight bow motion, then continued, "He's the one that taught me ta read. Said ya couldn't be anythin' in life if'n ya didn' know how ta read." Patty jerked the horses' reins to gently coax them into a gallop.

"Patty, if I'm being too personal, tell me; but how did your mother get the money to bring both of you over here?"

"Aye, have ya ever hern of indentured servant? Me ma signed papers to work for Mr. Webster fer five years fer free if'n me college was paid fer. He agreed, but he likes hern so much, 'e let hern off the agreement, so she could earn hern own money to take care of us. I'll pay him back when I gets me doctorate, which I will," Patty stated with conviction, and then he was quiet again.

"I've seen the wealthy people take advantage of the Irish, how they get them to sign indentured papers and never release them, almost enslaving them. From what I've seen, the Irish are hard workers. It's a shame."

"Aye, they're 'ard workers, though not many of 'em are educated. They come 'ere not knowin' ta read er write, 'n can't fin' work. So they gets depressed and drink too much, but me thinks it is 'cause they aren't educated. If ye can't read er write, how ye figure 'ow ta do things? I 'av seen many boys take ther own lives, watched me best pardner hangin' from a tree; 'twas a cryin' shame. I was thinkin' maybe we can make friends with some of da bubs, like

43

Edith Gleason

teachers such as yournself, and we could 'elp the Irish learn 'ow ta read." Patty spoke with passion and concern, and his eyes lit up at the idea of helping his people.

"I concur, Patty. That's a great idea. We could use the church as a meeting place and maybe get some of the townspeople to contribute supplies. I have some of my own supplies that I've been collecting, and I could donate some of those too. I'll talk to my Uncle Jim. He's got a pretty close relationship with the pastor, so that should help. Oh, this is exciting!" Angel clasped her hands together and giggled.

Patty too was excited about this new project. "When da ya think we should get started?"

"I'll start tonight by asking my uncle, and then tomorrow at school I'll tell you the outcome. I expect it to be good news, so don't go fretting. After that, I need to get started on some of my course work. I'll have to start my research on my term paper. I've been putting it off until the last minute, but I think it finally caught up to me."

"What's yourn term paper about?"

"Professor Jordan wants us to write how the gunslingers' ways have affected society and our way of life in the west, if they have stunted our progress, and finally if they'll continue to haunt the west. I've chosen Wild Bill Hickok for my paper. It should prove to be interesting. I'll let you read it when I'm finished."

"Sounds great, I'd like ta know the history 'bout America."

Both young people sat quietly in thought for the rest of the ride home. Patty reined in the horses and stopped to let Angel out in front of the brownstone.

"I want to thank you for picking me up and to let you know if it ever interferes with anything you have to do, please just let me know and I'll get another ride," Angel said, looking at Patty.

"Aye, ye know I will. For now, 'tis workin' out great, yer bringin' the lunch, 'n me the ride. I'll be seein' ye, Miss Angel." He clicked his tongue and was off.

That night was the beginning of Angel and Patty fulfilling a need and a dream for the Irish immigrants. Angel put her plans on paper,

44

and Patty organized the schooling in his head and repeated it for Angel. It was going to be a huge undertaking, but one they thought together they could accomplish.

Chapter Ten

Angel was excited; after talking to the pastor of Uncle Jim's church, she and Patrick set up classes for the Irish immigrants.

"The church would be more than willing to help," the pastor stated. "You couldn't be an American, yet not see the plight of the immigrants."

"Yes, me an' Angel agree with ye. Teachin' 'em how ta read, if'n ye pardon the pun, will give 'em a leg up. And everyone needs ta 'ave equal standin'," Patty said excitedly. Looking over at Angel, he noticed that her thumb on both hands poked out through the two fingers of her fists, which she held close to her sides. He smiled.

"We could hold class every Tuesday night in the church at seven p.m.," Angel added.

"It sounds to me as if you two young people have put a lot of thought into this endeavor of yours already. You have my blessings. If there is anything else I can help with, let me know."

"We do." Laughing out of sheer pleasure, the pastor took several of the flyers. "Is there anything else, before I go?"

"No thank you, Pastor. You've helped so much," Angel said.

"I'll be expecting you in church on Sunday. Don't let me down. Good Day." Pastor tipped his hat and went on his way.

Patty spoke as they hurried on their way, "We can make a few stops on our way and nail some to the trees in the city, and I'll give some to me cousins to pass 'round. We should 'ave a good turnout."

News of the classes spread like wildfire, and on their first night twenty Irish immigrants were in attendance.

"Oh, Patrick, look how God blesses us!"

"Aye, I'll give 'em da credit since it 'twas yourn church dat 'elped." Patrick looked down and saw how Angel held her hands again. "What is dat all 'bout?" He reached out and tapped her fists.

Angel looked at her own fists and smiled. "You know I had never noticed that I did that until recently, but I figured out why. Ever since my baby brother passed on, I curl my fingers around my thumbs and it comforts me. It almost feels as if someone is holding

46

my hands, helping me go through a hard time. I know it's the Lord because he promised to never leave us nor forsake us, and that's my way of keeping him close." Angel looked pleased as she watched the new students file in and seat themselves.

Patrick stared out across the room and marveled at his thought, *Who is this God, that he could hold your hand?*

Together they both decided that it was going to be a lot of work, but they knew it would be worth it.

*****

After three months, they watched their class size grow as students came and went, all for good reasons. More and more of their students acquired jobs. Angel picked a student that would assist her in her teaching, Nellie. She was a quick study and grasped the English language quickly.

Everything about her was Irish, from her red hair to her green eyes and finally her fair skin. She was an eager student and was always willing to help. It was apparent to everyone that she had a crush on Patrick, so, of course, that made her a little more willing to help.

Patrick began to notice Nellie one day. "Aye, Patrick, do ye feel like 'tis too hot in 'ere?" Nellie reached for her braid and, loosening her hair, shook it loose and let it fall softly to her waist. She looked at Patrick, and the look of enthrallment he gave pulled a giggle from Nellie. Patrick's cheeks and ears turned red.

After that, Nellie always had a smile for Patty; and he always had one for Nellie. Nellie would laugh at every joke he made, even if it wasn't funny. After a few weeks of so much given and received attention, they began to date.

"Patty, I canno' reach the shelf where da books are. Can ye 'elp me?" Nellie batted her eyes and, slowly swishing her skirt close to him, touching his arm gently, she smiled up at him.

"Aye, ye know I can. I woudna want ta 'ave ye fallin, Luv."

Angel found it endearing and cute how both would banter and flirt. Nellie went with Patrick everywhere. For the longest time they seemed like two peas in a pod.

47

Edith Gleason

One day Nellie approached Angel, "I think me Patty is goin' ta ask me ta marry 'im. I thinks I'm goin' ta say yes."

"Are you asking me if it's okay, Nellie?" Angel was surprised.

"Aye, I am, since it be ye dat saw 'im first."

"It's not who saw him first, but who he loves. I've seen the way he caters to you and watches your every move. He's never left your side since the day you both met. If you're asking me, I'd say he only has eyes for you," Angel assured her.

Nellie blushed and smiled at the same time, "Yourn just bein' kind, Miss Angel, but I thank ye for it. Don't tell 'im I said anythin' to ye, please."

"My lips are sealed. He won't hear anything from me." They both giggled as Patty stepped inside the room with an armload of books.

"Am I ta think ye was talkin' 'bout me?" Both of the girls shook their heads.

"Never. We would never talk about you, Patty." Patrick just playfully shook his head, gave them a look of disbelief and then went about placing the books in their proper places.

Every other week all three of them would sit down after class and figure out their curriculum and their plans for the students. That gave Angel time to do school studies that, as of late, she had let slide a bit.

Patty spent a lot of his free time in the pubs with his cousins and fellow policemen. They would drink more and more lagers 'til one or all of them would pass out. It was beginning to affect Patrick's schooling and Angel and Nellie could see it. The girls decided that it was time to have a talk with Patty. Sitting down one night after school had let out, they began.

"Patty, you're not going out again tonight with yourn buds, are you? You 'ave been comin' back so late. I'm feared for yourn schoolin'. How ya goin' ta be a sawbones ifn ye don't get yer schoolin' in?" Nellie had been the first to speak.

Patty looked at her in surprise, "I've taken keer of me self 'til now. I don't think I'll be needin' another Ma, but thanks."

"Patrick, she only speaks out of concern, and so do I. You've

48

come so far, and to just let it all go for a few drinks or lagers doesn't make much sense," Angel pleaded.

"What doesn't make much sense is ta have two women naggin' me 'bout my business. I can take keer of me self without any help from anyone. I took keer of me ma and me self back then, and I can do the same 'ere."

"Oh Patrick, without the Lord you could drink yourself into oblivion and never come out of it. Then you would wake up lost not just because of the drink, but because of your choice not to know the Lord. He's just a prayer away, Patty," Angel was still pleading.

"He could be right here now, but I'm not ready. I understand what yourn tryin' ta do fer me. Ya want me ta 'ave a 'appy life and a 'appy e'er after. Yourn a good friend, Angel; and I loves ya too, Nellie, fer carin' that much 'bout me. Today is just not that day. Someday I will, but not today. I 'ear what yourn sayin' 'bout the lagers, 'n I think yourn both right. I'll slow me self down from ta drink and spend more time with me Nellie. Does that be suitin' ya ladies?" Patrick said, smiling his biggest smile. "Course I'll 'ave to es-plain to me pardners tonight, but I won't partake of the liquor."

"Aye, Patty, me love. Ya make me so proud. Will ye be wantin' to walk me home tonight?" Nellie's head was bent in a shy gesture.

"Aye, I'd be wantin' ta walk ya home. Are we settled up 'ere, Angel?" Patty had turned his attention towards Angel.

"Yes, Patty, you and Nellie have a nice walk home; and I'll see you tomorrow, God willing that the Creeks don't rise."

"What?" Patrick and Nellie queried.

"Oh sorry, it's just a saying that we say when we can't be positive about something, but I'll see ya. Goodnight." Angel laughed and with that all three went out the door and went their separate ways. They would see each other tomorrow, God willing.

Edith Gleason

Chapter Eleven

Angel went to the library in town and also to the local newspapers to gather information for her term paper on gunslingers of the west. She was surprised at how much information there was on Wild Bill Hickok.

Delving into her studies, she read the papers. The first paper she read was an article from *The Atchison Daily Champion*. It stated how Wild Bill at that time worked for the railroad and how the McCanles gang had come to burn down the station at which Wild Bill worked. During the fight, Wild Bill shot McCanles through the heart with his rifle and then, stepping out the door, finished the other two off with his revolver. A fourth one he wounded—who ran off, never to be heard from again.

Angel gathered up some more news articles about Wild Bill and jotted down what she could find. *The Brownsville Advertiser* told of how, during the distribution of arms and ammunition, there was a dispute, and a rope was put around a Union man's neck (Wild Bill); and he was dragged for a long while, then hoisted to a tree to hang. The man escaped to a house where he was hunted. The situation commenced into a gunfight in which three of the men were killed while the other two hastily retreated.

Next she read an account of Wild Bill in *The Missouri Weekly Patriot*. It stated how Wild Bill had been employed in government service as a scout, a guide and as a part of exploration parties. Many of the commanding officers testified about his actions. Wild Bill shot and killed David Tutt in the town square over a card game. Later she read of the trial they gave him for that killing and that he was found not guilty by the jury in just ten minutes.

Harper's New Monthly Magazine described Wild Bill's attributes. They claimed he had clear grey eyes and he stood six-foot-one inches tall, had a large strong chest, and a small round waist where he carried two Colt's navy revolvers..

Angel read further and found the description of Wild Bill somewhat endearing.

50

After the Rains

As a Rough Rider, when asked if it was alright to print an article about him, he teared up and asked that they make sure to mention that he had fought through the war for the Union like a true man. He also told them he hadn't seen his mother in many a year and that he loved her more than anything in this life. Now she was old and feeble, but hearing that about him would make her proud.

The St. Louis Missouri Democrat reported him as being handsome. They stated he carried himself straight up, was free from blemish with a small moustache, grey-blue eyes, and hair parted down the middle with long curly black locks hanging behind his ears. His language was good and he boasted of college learning. He was generous to the point of extravagance.

When asked how many white men he had killed, to his knowledge, he replied, "Near a hundred, but none without just cause." When asked about his first kill, he told them about the time he was in Leavenworth City. He had noticed some unsavory characters walking about, so he reserved a room for the night. He had retired for the night and had only lain about thirty minutes when he heard men at his door. So he readied himself with his pistol and his knife; having them half-concealed, he feigned sleep.

He said five men entered the room and whispered about killing him. He said he kept still until the knife touched his breast, and then he sprung to the side killing one and wounding another. He gathered some soldiers and rounded up fifteen men in all. When they searched the basement, they found the remains of eleven men that had been murdered. He then asked, "Wouldn't you have done the same?" Then he finished with, "That was the first man I killed, and I've never been sorry about it."

Angel finished the articles, and then replaced them in their perspective places. She sat back and reread what she had found and then writing down her thoughts, she began…

"Wild Bill Hitchcock, is he a hero or a gunslinger? From the information that I've been able to gather from what was available about this man, it appears that maybe he was closer to a hero. A misdirected Union man that tended to take the law into his own hands, yet in the end the result would have been the same from a jury.

51

Edith Gleason

"Sometimes what you see in a person isn't always what they are. Did this gunslinger hurt our society or add to it? I can only say that someone has to take a stand for what is right and what is wrong, whether it be a lawman or a citizen. In the end we stand before God and answer for all that we've done. We alone present our best and only case.

"Society is formed from all kinds of men and women: the good and the bad, the righteous and the unholy. But who is it that decides what is what, Men? I believe gunslingers are a part of our history. Will they always be there? I believe in some form or another, there will always be the lawless. It may not be a gun they hold, but there will be dishonesty. They may not steal your breath, but they can steal your life. I believe from our history comes our future. For myself, let me be a good steward with what God has given me and make the future look more promising and less lawless."

Angel sat back and read her paper. She hoped the professor would like it. She would hand it in on Monday to Professor Jordan, and until then she would finish her other studies. It was getting late and she was tired.

*****

Monday morning came, and Angel handed her paper in early at the start of class. Professor Jordan approached her after the bell. "Excuse me, Angel; I've read your paper and found it very insightful. I'm actually surprised that you gave me that much effort. I hear tell that many professors don't think women can handle an education; too much studying would cause them to faint. I see you're up and about, and it didn't take too much out of you," Professor Jordan said with a bit of a sly smile and a wink.

"Thank you, Professor Jordan, your opinion means a lot to me. No, I didn't faint in the process of research and reading. As far as I know, I still have my wits about me. I take it you don't agree with the findings of these scholars and their opinions about women and education?"

"No, I don't agree, and you're not the first educated woman I've met. It's always a pleasure to meet another. So you're going to be a teacher? You might be aware that you're entering a man's field of work. You're not going to get paid what you're worth, but you stick to it; and eventually they'll see what a rare find they have. You're a strong, persistent young woman; and I admire that and, as far as I can tell, I think you'll succeed at anything you put your mind to."

"Thank you again, Professor Jordan, and may I say that I also am an admirer of anyone that can teach *to* a person and not *at* a person. You make it personal. I enjoy your lectures and your classes."

"Well, I guess that's enough of patting each other's backs. You hang in there, Angel. God will use you for his greater purpose; I believe that. It's been a pleasure." At that same time Patrick rounded the corner to hurry to lunch. Nellie was joining them today, and he didn't want to miss her.

Chapter Twelve

"Now that I'm an intern sawbones, I have orders to leave for London, where I'll be finishin' me studies. Nellie will be meetin' me over there in the fall, and I would like if'n ye come with me, Angel. Yourn just like me sis, and I could use yourn strength and friendship. England is a big place. I'd feel lost without ya." Patrick was anxious. "I hope you agree to go with me. Ye can 'ave a career teaching in London. There's much more people in da world than in Montana." Angel knew she couldn't go with him. So instead she tried to encourage him with other things, starting with Nellie.

"Nellie will be there with you. I'm positive that together England won't seem so big. Imagine what two people could do. I think you two were meant for each other. I want it so that you're not hurt; but I'm sorry, Patrick. Since you last asked me to consider it, I've given it lots of thought and prayer, really I have; and I still feel God is calling me to teach in Montana. I can't be in England and Montana at the same time, but I can promise that someday I'll visit you."

"God, what has God got to do with it? If he's real, he'll go wherever you go. There are uneducated children there too. Think of the good you could do there. Ye can save the children some other place in the world. As far as Nellie goes, leave hurn ta me."

"Oh, Patrick, it's not that I want to save the world's children; it's because my Heavenly Father is telling me I'm needed in Montana. Jesus already saved the world."

"Aye, in yourn book, not mine. Are ye sure this Casey ye talked 'bout so often isn't the real reason ye don't want ta go?"

"Patrick, I don't know how to answer that. I've thought about it; but I'm sure he must be in a relationship by now, so that pretty much does away with any thoughts of Casey, other than as a friend. I could never hurt him. No, I have no other reason except that I just trust the Lord, and where he leads I'll follow."

Angel's tone softened, "Patrick, your life could be so different. It grieves my heart so that you will not trust the Lord with your life, especially now that you and Nellie are to marry. He knows your name, and every hair on your head is numbered. He knew you in your mother's womb; and, ever since, he's so been waiting for you."

"Aye, don't worry, lass." The remorse he felt for hurting her showed in his eyes. Patty reached out and traced her chin, then wiped the tears that had begun to form and drop to her cheeks. He spoke soothingly, "I'll believe in him someday, Angel; but today is not that day."

"Don't wait too late, Patrick, please."

Dismissing the subject, he looked away and continued, "So ye won't be goin' with me on the great ship. I'll miss ye, my wee sweet lass, 'n I will always love ye, my sister."

"Yes, I'll always love you too, my brother; and I'll keep praying for you always." Patty was in love with Nellie, but Angel was special to him. He pulled Angel close and kissed her as gently as he could, even though down to the very core of his being, he wanted to hold onto her forever and take her with him. He released her reluctantly; and with a smile and a nod, he turned and walked as stormily out of her life as he had walked in. Only this time he wasn't breaking up a fight; he was battling the war within himself.

Angel stood quietly weeping and watching until she could see his figure no more, then asked God to watch over her best friend and the love of his life, Nellie, when she too would take her leave. She would miss him greatly but resigned herself to continue to pray for Patrick, her adopted wayward brother. Sadly she turned and walked into the house and let the door quietly close behind her.

*****

The town of Manchester had paid Patty's way to England and reserved a small building where he was to be the town's resident doctor. Patty set to work as soon as his feet touched the soil of Manchester. He didn't have many slow days; but this day he didn't have any patients scheduled, so he decided to get to know his neighborhood. He walked among rows of back-to-back housing, noticing each house had a front entrance only; and there were six bathrooms for every forty houses.

The raw sewage filled the streets, and the stench was so strong it made Patrick gag. He wondered how the people here managed to

55

exist without some kind of disease. Patty had already witnessed the disease of deformity in young children. They worked such long hours in the mills and factories that it caused their tender young bones to cripple them. His heart ached for them, and he knew then that his calling would be to help the children in the workhouses. There had to be an answer to child labor; "for every step forward, there is always a step backward," he noted to himself.

Returning to his practice, he sat down at his desk in the back room, which served as his home, and began to write.

My Darling Nellie,

It is with love and a heart full of yearning ta see that beautiful face of yourn, so I can tell ya that I've booked a passage aboard a freighter ta go back ta home so we can be married. Then I can bring me beautiful bride to be by my side. I'm busy here, and I sure could use yer help with me patients. 'Specially the wee ones, I knows ye 'ave a heart for the children. There is so much help they be needin', and yer just great with kids.

I'm comin' home fer ye, Nellie.

All o' me heart, Patty!

Patty reread the letter, then placed it in an envelope, sealed it with a kiss and began his next letter.

Dearest Angel,

I've found where I belong. I believe if you could see what I've seen, you would think yourn calling was here too. I'm still hoping ya change yer mind. The poor here are put into poor houses, and the children are sent to work in the mills 'n factories. They start at age eight and when they reach thirteen, they are crippled. It breaks yer heart.

I've booked passage on a boat, and I'm comin' back to America. I'm going ta marry Nellie and try to talk ye into comin' back with us. Are ye still praying for me? I knows ye are, Thanks!

Hope to see all yourn friendly faces soon.

Yourn friend, Patty!

Patrick packed his belongings and put a sign on his front window explaining his departure and when he hoped he would return. Locking the door, he looked sadly at the surroundings, "Aye, if I were a prayin' man, I'd be askin' da Lord fer some help."

Patty boarded the ship and shook the captain's hand, "Aye, Captain, I be a sawbones if ya needin' any of me help." He smiled his engaging smile and the Captain nodded his agreement.

After not too long aboard, Patty was being shaken inside the hull of the ship. Grabbing onto his bunk, he tried to steady himself. Finally, unable to sleep from the commotion, he roused and, clinging to the sides of the keel, made his way up to the bow.

"Aye, Captain," he shouted above the billowing wind and crashing waves. "Are we goin' ta make it?"

The Captain, holding on to the stern, shouted back, "I hope you're a praying man."

There was no moonlight on this night, only the glitter from the lanterns that shone out from below deck; and it was also reflected in the rain that poured down.

Then there on a great ship in the throes of an Atlantic storm, there knelt a young Irish man, praying out loud to the Heavenly Father, "Aye, ye know me. I believe in ye, an' I'll be needin' forgiveness from ye for all that I done. I'm not a knuck or a bad sort, just don' know what ta believe. I know ye now. If Angel and Nellie can be loved by ye, then I want to be loved by ye. Yourn Bible says ye saved the world, so I be askin' ye to save me soul; I'll be yourn 'til I die and, because of Heaven, I'll be yourn there too. Thank ye, Jesus, and would ye mind letting me Nellie and mine ma know that I'll be seein' 'em..."

It was at that precise moment that the fierce waves of the Atlantic Ocean crashed over the ship and finished his prayer for him. As the great waters swept, it tore the now-splintered ship to the water, leaving nothing but emptiness in place of lives that were headed to a new beginning.

Patty was gone in an instant and had felt no pain, only a calm peace and glowing light that had been awaiting him. On top of a

Edith Gleason

piece of drifting wood that had once been part of the mast, a Bible lay.

Then torrents of water turned the Bible over, and it slowly sank into the deep, darkness of the water. Belongings and wood lay scattered about, floating and being pushed along with the waves.

Then slowly, piece by piece, sinking in the dark fathoms below, they began to fade from sight. And the place where a young Irish man—who had knelt and given his heart to the Lord—had been swept away by the crashing waves and ascended to heaven.

Psalms 103:15-16: "Man's life, like the flower of the field, so shall he flourish, but then the wind passes over it and it is gone and the place thereof, shall know it no more."

*****

A soft rap sounded at Jim's door, and he went to answer it. He opened the door to Patrick's mother, Mary. She wiped her eyes and spoke quietly, "I be likin' to talk to yourn Angel; I 'ave some news 'bout me Paddy." Jim became somber and respectfully ushered Angel and Mary into the parlor before leaving them to talk.

Angel spoke first, "What news do you have of Patrick, Mary? He's only been gone a month."

"Aye, I know. It's a short time, but now it be so long. I be sorry to tell ye, me Paddy...is no more. His ship went down on the Atlantic. They tell me there be no survivors. Just like his Da, me Paddy's ne'er comin' 'ome again." Mary dropped her head into her hands and began to weep.

Angel was speechless. Tears of grief quickly flowed down her cheeks. A man she loved like a brother had been taken from her. She grabbed at her chest, for her heart ached brutally; she thought she could hear it breaking; and, as she thought she could bear the pain no more, Mary's tears dripped on her hand and brought Angel back from her own grieving. She asked the Lord for strength and then reached out to console Mary.

She gathered the older woman in her arms like a small broken child. Together they talked into the early morning hours. They talked of all the good times they had spent with Patrick, and together they mourned one of earth's lost creatures. Angel prayed with Mary and assured her Patrick was in heaven. For some reason Angel felt comfort from the Lord that Patty did make it to heaven and even now was watching over them.

Chapter Thirteen

The wake for Patty took place on Sunday morning in the very place that he and Angel had taught the immigrants. Patty's ma wanted it at her home, but changed her mind after she found out how many students wanted to pay their last respects.

Looking around and noticing all the gaiety and laughter that the Irish called a wake, Angel still found sadness. She walked among all of them and would sometimes politely step out of the way as they lifted their lagers to Patrick with talk and memories of time spent with him, some of which she also shared. All of Patty's friends gave a toast to Patty, and one in particular Angel thought was fitting, "The work praises the man."

Another was given, "Both your friend and your enemy think you will never die." A man with his lager rose to speak as well, "May the light of Heaven shine on yourn grave."

Then the room quieted when Nellie took her place up front and began her soft send-off to her dearly departed,

May the good earth be soft under you,
When you rest upon it.
'N may it rest easy over you when,
At last you lay out under it.
'N may it rest so lightly over you,
That your soul may be out quickly,
And up, and off,
And be on its way to God.
God bless ye, Patty, I'll always love ye.

Nellie forced a smile through her agony as her eyes started to drip the tears she could no longer contain. Then, wiping her cheeks, she made her way quickly to the back of the room and quietly sat in a chair next to Mary. It was Angel's turn now, so she made her way to the front and began:

"I'm not Irish; but, given the choice, I'd decide to be born of that descent. What makes me say that is all of the good Irish people I've met and had the pleasure to know. You are the hardest working and most fun-loving people that I've ever met. I'm proud to be among you all, yet even prouder to have known Patty. He was a dreamer and a hero. He didn't just imagine a thing; he put his feet to his dreams, and that is what made him a hero. His Uncle Scott gave me an Irish prayer; and because it is fitting for this occasion, I'd like to read it to you now, for Patty." Angel cleared her voice and began:

"Do not stand at my grave and weep,
I am not there…I do not sleep.
I am the thousand winds that blow,
I am the diamond glitz on snow.
I am the sunlight on ripened grain,
I am the gentle autumn rain.
When you wake in the mornings hush,
I am the swift uplifting rush,
Of gentle birds in circling flight,
I am the soft star that shines at night.
Do not stand at my grave and cry -
I am not there…I did not die."

Angel dropped her head and wiped her eyes, then lifted her head and finished, "I too will always love Patty, and I believe that he is in heaven now. So I offer up another saying in honor of my friend, 'May the smile of God light you to glory.' I love you, Patty."

The room whooped and hollered and lifted their lagers with cheers for one of their best buds. The wake lasted past dawn, but Angel and Nellie had retired hours before and grieved for Patty in their own way with prayer and many tears.

*****

Angel continued her studies with the Irish immigrant people up until it was time for her graduation. Nellie was more than capable of teaching the people, and she had taken over all of the teaching duties.

"Ah yes, I still mourn me Patrick, but I try to do everything as unto the Lord. I know'd if he was 'ere, he would be proud of me."

61

Edith Gleason

Nellie spoke as she and Angel finished up their lunch on the park bench.

"I've watched you teach and grow in the Lord, Nellie, and you just amaze me. I think that Patrick would be proud of you too. Are you still coming over to the house so we can go over some lessons?"

"Aye, that's the plan," Nellie answered with a smile. Angel and Nellie had become great friends since Patrick's passing. Nellie visited Uncle Jim's home quite a bit. They spent their time laughing, talking and reminiscing about Patrick.

One night, quite unexpectedly, Nellie surprised Angel with a gift. "Here, me Angel," Nellie said, withdrawing a picture from her pocket. "A street photographer took it when me Patrick and I were walkin' 'bout. He's beautiful, in't he?" Nellie proclaimed wistfully.

Angel took the picture and, as if it were fragile, held it carefully in her hands. She traced Patrick's face gently, "Yes, he is beautiful and he was so smart."

"Aye, and me thinks the angels are fawning over him too." Nellie sniffled and smiled as she became a bit glossy.

"And I think Patrick is enjoying the attention." They looked at each other in agreement and laughed, and then Angel placed her new treasure carefully between the pages of her Bible. "There," she said, "Once again he's in God's hands."

"God bless 'im," offered Nellie; then both of the young women went back to their work.

As time for going home grew closer, Angel gave the supplies to Nellie that she needed and promised to pray for God to guide her. Nellie assured that she'd write often when she got home. Not only did Nellie learn to speak English; but she'd also learned to write and read it, plus she had accepted the Lord into her heart as well.

Angel thought back to the time of Nellie's conversion. She was definitely Irish in her joy as she grabbed her dress and danced the jig, whooping and hollering, "Ah, Lord I love ye! Thank ye, Father, for lovin' me!" She was overjoyed and claimed she had never felt such love or been so loved. Everything had taken on a new freshness. Angel would never forget her words, "Oh, Angel, if I only could a'member what 'twas like ta be born, I'd think 'twas truly like a newness in me of being born again."

Angel considered it pure pleasure to watch Nellie grow in the Lord and watch the star in her eyes become the light to her soul. Angel enjoyed the friendships she had garnered since her arrival in Boston. Thinking of them now made her a little sorry that she would soon be leaving.

The last day they spent together, Angel made a promise, "I'll write every chance I get to see how things are going with your teachings. I'm going to miss you so much, Nellie; it already hurts."

"Ah me Angel, God's word says he takes keer of our tomorrows. Don't be frettin' o'er me. If'n ye thinks it's a man I be needin', don't ye worry. I've had me eye on Donovan. Do ya 'member him–tall, dark and handsome? He's no Patty, but he's sweet 'n he's sweet on me."

Nellie giggled. "I'll be prayin' God fills your hurt with gladness and laughter 'cause that's the best medicine. I'll throw a man in there too, can't hurt." Then Nellie reached out and gave her friend a big hug. That helped Angel feel better about her leaving; but just the same, she would still miss her newfound friends.

Chapter Fourteen

Angel had been gone for about a year and three months, so she decided she would write another letter to Casey and her family. Just as she was sitting down to start, Aunt Lorraine appeared at her door with letters from home.

"Not one, but three letters?" Angel read the postmarks and senders. "Langley Williams." *Why would he be writing me? Oh well, I'll open his first,* she thought. Getting comfortable on her divan, she began to read.

Dear Miss Angel;

I have been informed that my business travels will include Boston at Christmas time. My thoughts are as follows. I'd be much obliged if you would accompany me to the theatre and dinner. I can guarantee your safety in the city and that you would thoroughly enjoy yourself. If you have no reservations about these plans, then I will take no response as a "yes," and I will show up at your door on Christmas Eve or there about.

Sincerely and with best wishes,

Langley Williams.

Angel lay down the letter next to her and gave it a serious thought. "I don't see any harm in spending some time with a friendly acquaintance or, for that matter, a childhood friend." He was always so serious in his manner. Even as a child, one didn't hear too much laughter from him, and his letter still dictated that kind of demeanor. Angel remembered him as a child in what seemed like a lifetime ago now.

"Come on, Langley. Most kids squeal like a pig when they're getting tickled," Casey dropped his hands and looked bewilderedly at Langley.

"Father says laughter is for the simple-minded and that I shouldn't laugh, lest I be considered one of them."

"Well, all I can say is you must be strong," Casey muttered.

64

"You know, Langley, the Bible says that 'A merry heart doeth like good medicine,'" Angel said, trying to encourage Langley to have fun.

"Well, Father says that there is no such thing as God so that makes the Bible a fairy tale. We don't read it." Langley was staunch in his beliefs. Casey and Angel were taken aback.

After a few minutes, Angel said softly, "That's alright, Langley. It doesn't matter what you believe; we still love you," She watched as his face softened, and he followed the small group to the river for continued play. Angel's thinking was that maybe their time together would benefit him. Langley needed to smile and not just over business.

"Well, that settles that. No response required," Angel smiled to herself.

Then she picked up the letter from Momma. Angel tried to be gentle, but she couldn't contain her excitement. Her fingers shook as she tore open the first letter and began to read,

Our Darling Angel,

How are you doing? We pray for you every day. We miss you very much. We loved the letters from your travels. It sounded beautiful and made us feel as if we were with you. Your brothers say, "Howdy." They tell me they miss teasing you and mussing up your hair. Papa wants to know if you're keeping up with your Bible reading and prayers. He said that's the staples that get you through life.

Papa bought fifty more head of cattle, so he had to hire on more ranch hands. He made Wes head over the other hands. From what papa tells me, Wes has been building his own house. I guess he can't live here forever.

Toby has found himself a love. Her name is Jeanette. She's beautiful. She's tall with long brown hair and green eyes. Toby proposed last week and she accepted! They're to be married before Christmas. It will be nice to have another daughter for me and a new sister for you.

Tim and Andrew couldn't be outdone; they have also been dating

a couple of girls pretty steadily. Tim has his Andrea, and Andrew has his Lisa. Both girls are giving them a run for their lives. It makes it interesting around here.

Carson still enjoys his horses and fishing. Casey takes him fishing down by the old river sometimes, and they go watch Wes and Billy race on Saturdays. (I know you used to like to do that when you were home.) Casey is like an older brother to Carson, always teaching him things and watching over him, of course. Rachael is always in attendance with Casey. I think he's serious about her. Carson says that Casey is going away to college too. Just not as far away as you are. I know Carson will miss him.

I entered my cherrie pie at the fair this summer. It won! Papa said he wasn't surprised, but I was. There are so many good cooks here. Since you're not here, next time I make one, I'll eat a piece for you.

I'm going to close now. Write and tell us how school is and life with Uncle Jim, Aunt Lorraine and Lyndee. Tell them we said, "Hi" and to come see us one day. We all love you, Angel, and are praying for you.

Love Always,
Momma and Papa, Toby, Tim, Andrew and Carson Winters

Wow, Angel thought, *she had never imagined her brothers getting married and moving away.* These new changes made Angel a little blue. She knew that nothing stayed the same and that everything happens for a purpose, but she wasn't prepared for her family to change just yet.

Angel looked down at the other letter in her hand; it was from Casey. She opened it and began to read,

Dear Angel,

It seems like forever since I've seen you. Have you changed much? I've gotten taller and maybe a little bigger, at least in the shoulder area. Your brothers tease me and tell me my head has gotten bigger too since I have enrolled in college.

I didn't tell you that, did I? I'll be going to ministerial school.

66

I've always felt the call to be a minister. I don't think God will mind the mischievous side of me. After all, he created me. I'll be certified by the time you come home, and I'll be looking for a church. I just might have to build one.

I sure do miss you. Are you enjoying Boston? Is it very different from home? By the way, Wes is the top contender in the horse races. I guess he'll be joining the horse racing circuit before long. He's dating a girl whose father breeds horses. There's nothing like having your choice of a steed, and a winning one at that.

It's sad, but I think Wes has joined the wrong crowd. A bunch of rowdy cowboys came to town for a seasonal round up; and from what I've seen, they're heavy drinkers and into gambling. Wes has been arrested for drunken and disorderly conduct. I hear your Father is thinking of letting him go. I think he could use some prayers.

Carson and I have been fishing a lot. Your momma even cooked up the last lot of fish we caught, and, boy, they were good. She even showed me how to cook them. When you come home, Carson and I will have to cook you our special fish dinner. He misses you too, by the way.

I guess Momma Cat has already told you that I'm dating Rachael. Her father also happens to be the dean at the college I attend. She's quite the looker and nice too. I think she's a little more serious than I am, though, as if I could be serious.

I hear your cousin Lyndee has taken my place. I'll have to hear about some of your escapades with her, before I'll believe she has replaced me. I hope to see you at Christmas. God willing that the Creeks don't rise. Miss you a lot!!!

Your true friend,
Casey Jones

Angel folded the letter and placed it back in the envelope. Casey always made her smile. She wasn't surprised he was going to be a minister; he had a way of talking. So he had a steady girlfriend. *Good for him,* she thought, and yet her gut wrenched. Angel sighed; she missed him too and maybe more than she realized before now.

Another year and she would be going home as a teacher. It wasn't long, but it seemed so far away. Christmas was next month, and she wouldn't be there with her family. She had gathered trinkets for them throughout the year and had already shipped them home. She was going to miss momma's cherry pies and homemade gifts. Angel missed accompanying Papa and her brothers on their hunting trips through the snow, the search for that perfect Christmas tree. After sitting up the tree and trimming it, the family would stand side by side, singing around the piano as Papa played, "Oh holy night." The fire crackled in the hearth as the fire's heat from the chimney warmed the outside, and that their insides were warmed from the laughter that filled their home.

Angel was homesick. She opened her bureau drawer to put her letters away when her hand came across the diamond cameo that Langley had brought her.

He had sent a letter saying he would be in Boston at Christmas time, and he promised to stop by and see her. *It'll be nice to see someone from home,* she thought to herself. Angel bent her head and prayed for Langley. She prayed for his loneliness and direction, but most of all for his salvation.

Afterwards, she dropped her head back onto her pillow. So Wes is dating someone. She hadn't thought about him in a long while. Maybe time and distance had proven what Momma knew all along, "He isn't the one God has waiting for you." It was strange how Momma's words were almost audible to her ears even now and appropriate at this moment. Casey had a steady girl too; odd how that piece of news made her feel a little discouraged.

Chapter Fifteen

With a growing concern, Rachael stood quietly at the doorway and observed Casey. His back was to her as he sat at his desk penning another letter, which she could only assume was to Angel. For her, this was a subject that could no longer be avoided. She would broach the subject of Angel with him today, probably after dinner when they discussed the day's events.

Casey sat in deep thought. This had to be one of the hardest letters he had ever written to Angel. He questioned why that would be. He was only telling her of his impending wedding to Rachael; it was something he should be excited about and want to share with his best friend. Yet inside he felt torn, almost as if he had been unfaithful.

He shook his head to clear his mind of his last thought and instead put his thoughts on his future bride. She was intelligent, resourceful, easy on the eyes, and carried herself with grace. He loved to listen to her play the piano. When she touched the keys, she seemed to make each key sing its own song. She was talented in many areas and could put people at ease with her conversation.

Her looks were beyond the norm. She was tall and dignified, and she curled the ends of her strawberry blonde hair to let it fall about her shoulders. Her eyes were a bright green and one could easily lose oneself in them. She was the dean's daughter and had religious upbringing. So what was this uneasiness he felt as the wedding date drew closer? He sat lost in his own thoughts.

Rachael couldn't stand it any longer, nor could she pull herself away from this scene. She burst out, "Casey, what are you doing that is causing you to look so distressed?"

Casey was caught off-guard. He had no idea that Rachael had been standing there. "What? Do I look distressed?" he asked, surprised.

"Yes, your brows are furrowed, and your lips are drawn, pursed and thin. Aren't you writing a letter?"

"I was, but then I decided to put it off until later."

Edith Gleason

"Oh, and I can only assume it was another one to Angel. As a pastor, do you really think it's a good idea to continue this relationship you have with her?"

Casey protested, "What do you mean by that?"

Rachael rolled her eyes. "Casey, you of all people should know that there is no such thing as a friendship between a man and a woman. One of them always wants more. Which one are you?"

"How could you even ask me that? Did I not propose to you? Are we not getting married? What more could you need for proof of my commitment than that?" Casey was at a loss for understanding.

"I just need more than that! I need your eyes to light up when I walk into the room. I need you to embrace me and to need to kiss me with some kind of passion and desire." Rachael was frustrated and a bit disappointed.

Casey was exasperated, "If I didn't want you, I wouldn't have proposed to you."

"Wouldn't you have? Even if you thought the love of your life wasn't lost to you forever? I want to be more than second best. I won't settle for that and you shouldn't either."

"Am I your second best, Rachael?" he asked, confused.

"You are if you'd rather have someone else. I feel that because Angel was unattainable, you asked me," she replied quietly.

Casey's thoughts were racing. What did he feel? Were they both indeed settling for what was convenient and not for love? Casey sighed and pushed himself back in his chair.

"Is that how you see it, Rachael? Do you think I'm settling for second best?"

"Casey, that's not how I see it; that's how it is. I've tried to believe it would work anyways, with you being a pastor and all. But I am only fooling myself. You're still human, and you would never be happy with that kind of arrangement. Especially since your belief is that God directs our lives and chooses our loves," she stipulated.

"But Rachael … I've prayed about it, and you're perfect in every way a man could ever want," he pleaded.

"Maybe for some man I am perfect, but I don't think you are that man. I want more than just to be perfect to you; I want to be the only one

70

for you. I can see now that I am not. If you really thought about it, you would see that too. I believe that there is someone special that God chose just for me who will only think of me. I've waited and am willing to wait as long as it takes for that special someone. I think you need to talk to Angel and see if she's worth waiting for. As far as I'm concerned, this was all an illusion."

"So all of this comes down to you telling me you don't want to marry me." Casey was hurt. He felt confused, and he wasn't sure what he could or should do; but he didn't want to end things like this.

"It's not that I don't want to, it's that I'm not the one for you. I refuse to be anyone's second choice. I'm sorry."

Casey was quiet. He was saddened that Rachael thought that way but wasn't really sure if he felt the same. "Fine, Rachael; if I can't change your mind, then I'll do the necessary things to cancel the ceremony. Just know that I do love you. If you insist on this route, then yes, I'll use the time undoubtedly to figure things out. Admittedly I agree you deserve more out of a marriage. I'm sorry that it has to be this way between us, and I wish I could change it. I honestly feel that I love you, and I'm sorry if I led you to believe otherwise. If you change your mind, please let me know. I'll be here," Casey pleaded.

"You can't change things, Casey, mainly because God chooses when and whom you love. I'll gather some of my things that I have here and go home. I'll be having dinner with my father tonight. I'm sorry for the way things turned out, but it's all for the best. I want you to know that I have no regrets for any of it. And, Casey, I love you too, but sometimes it isn't enough just to love someone; it has to be reciprocated. In your quiet time, maybe you'll have an epiphany and see that I'm right. Remember God's word, 'Be still and know that I am God.' Goodbye, Casey."

Casey watched as Rachael left his life as quietly and gracefully as she had entered it. He didn't try to stop her. Somewhere deep inside him, confusion stirred and consequently he felt that maybe she *was* right.

He sat dejectedly at his desk, not knowing what to do. Then after hearing the latch on the front door as it closed, Casey dropped his

71

Edith Gleason

head in his hands and cried out to his Heavenly Father, "What kind of man am I to let a woman that loves me walk out of my life forever? Did you not guide me to her, Lord, or was she a distraction to keep me from being lonely? Oh Father, I've been chasing a dream of love for Angel. Will nothing ever come of it? Only you know, Lord. At this moment I ask for your comforting arms to surround Rachael and me. Lift us up and sustain us. We need it so. Help us both to find the loves of our lives, in your time, Father, not ours, Amen."

Casey finished with the assurance that his prayer would be answered. He knew the Bible said that the hairs on our heads are numbered and that the Heavenly Father watches over the sparrows, and how much greater are we that he takes care of our needs. The Bible assured him that he and Rachael would be taken care of.

Casey was saddened at this turn of events but comforted in knowing he was in the Father's hands. He stood and decided he would write Angel tomorrow. It was time to retire his mind and body, since it had been a very long and taxing day. He drew comfort from his faith in knowing God would take care of his tonight and all of his tomorrows.

Chapter Sixteen

It was Christmas morning and Aunt Lorraine had decorated the tree beautifully. Angel had missed not being able to participate, but Aunt Lorraine was a perfectionist. "If I let you girls help me, I'll be waiting until doomsday for it to be finished, too much frolicking and fooling around for me." Angel was sure that Aunt Lorraine had a point, but she missed helping out with the tree. So finally giving up, after a few unsolicited directions, the girls sat back, ate some of the popcorn, and enjoyed watching Aunt Lorraine do all the decorating.

The aroma of cinnamon and fruit in the homemade pies wafted through the air, making everyone feel hunger pains more acutely. Lyndee, in her own dramatic fashion, demonstrated her hunger by clutching her stomach and crawling to the sofa, while exclaiming she wasn't going to make it. She and Angel laughed.

Dinner was festive. They had invited people from church and the table was full. There was an array of foods lined in perfect order on the kitchen counter. It consisted of turkey and dressing, potatoes and yams, cranberry relish, corn and cornbread, and best of all pies. There were apple, blueberry, cherry and pumpkin. You could choose one, or some of all, which Lyndee did. It was a feast for the eyes, as well as the belly.

After dinner, Uncle Jim picked up his Bible, its cover worn from fingerprints and use. He then sat near the hearth and read aloud the story of Christ's birth. When it was time to open the gifts, Uncle Jim was pleased as he removed the wrapping of a large-print King James Bible, a gift from Angel.

His eyes misted over and, placing his forefinger on the Bible, he gently traced the words "Holy Bible" on the cover. Uncle Jim wasn't a preacher, but he loved to share God's word with others. When he was in church and got blessed, he would raise his hands in praise and give a shout. Angel was sure that in heaven, Uncle Jim would be in charge of the praise and shouting section. She could hear him now, "You there, brother in the back corner, lift up your hands and put a little more jump into that shout!" Angel smiled at the thought of it.

73

Edith Gleason

Everyone was pleased with the gift-giving and full from the wonderful dinner. They were all settling in the family room when a knock came at the door.

"Who could that be on Christmas day?" Uncle Jim asked as he rose from his warm chair. When he opened the door, it was a guest that was unfamiliar to everyone except Angel. A quiet reserved Langley stood before them with a wrapped gift in his hands, which he extended to Angel.

"Merry Christmas, everyone... Angel, this is for you."

Angel had already risen when she recognized who it was. Taking the package, she then meekly offered, "Thank you, Langley, and a merry Christmas to you also. Please, come in! If I had known you were coming bearing gifts, I would've prepared myself. I'm sorry, but I don't have a gift for you."

"I didn't expect a gift in return, but the thought is appreciated," he smiled.

Angel turned toward her already eavesdropping family. "Everyone, this is a friend of mine from Montana. Please meet Mr. Langley Brown."

Lyndee had already jumped to her feet at the first sight of a young man. The thought occurred to her that here is someone she hadn't flirted with yet. "Yes, please come in and sit down, Langley. How long have you been in town? How long are you staying? You know, Angel told us you were coming, but she didn't mention how good-looking you were."

Lyndee was able to ask every question within a matter of a few minutes. The same amount of time it took her to gently pull him by his arm to the sofa.

Langley's face reddened. Lyndee had a way of doing that to people. He got over his initial shock and sat down to talk of his travel and the business which had brought him to Boston. He found that he actually enjoyed Lyndee's attention and conversation. Still, he had an agenda, and his eyes drifted often toward Angel; and when Angel caught him, she would just smile.

"What are you doing tomorrow, Angel?" Langley asked on his way out the door. "I'd really like to take you to the vaudeville show they have here; I hear it's quite entertaining. After, if you like, I'd like you to accompany me to dinner at one of the fine restaurants. I'll be in town until the end of the week, and I'd like to see you as much as I can."

Angel didn't know what to say, except "yes." Since she'd received his letter, she had discussed it with her uncle and he approved. She longed to hear about home and the goings-on there. So she agreed to the 6 p.m. show; and as far as dinner went afterwards, she knew her uncle would say "no," since her only accompaniment was a young man. At the door she held out a small gift box.

"Here, maybe you could take some of Miss Jessie's confectionaries with you as a Christmas gift to enjoy on your return trip to your hotel room," she offered.

Langley smiled politely and accepted her gift. They said "Goodnight," and Angel stood on her toes to kiss him on the cheek; but Langley quickly turned his face so that their lips met instead. Angel, in truth, was astounded as he kissed her and held onto her longer than she thought a gentleman should have. Finally he released her and set her back on her feet.

"I'm sorry; I just missed you so very much. Please forgive me. I hope you're not offended and that you'll still go with me tomorrow."

Angel blushed; she had never been kissed before and just to be grabbed without permission had overwhelmed her a bit. She gathered her wits and tried to understand that maybe that's all it was, just innocent emotion, and he did say he was sorry.

"Yes, of course," she said. "You're forgiven. Tomorrow at 6:00 will be fine. Goodnight, Langley." He nodded and she closed the door softly.

His kiss had left her somewhat confused. Angel mulled it over in her mind as she walked up the stairs to her room. She decided she would pray about it and ask the Lord to calm her and give her understanding. This was something new that she hadn't expected, especially from Langley. Before closing the door behind her, she reached up and touched her lips where his had just been. She giggled in a girlish way before latching the knob shut.

*****

At 5:30 Angel was ready for her date. At the coaxing of her cousin Lyndee, she was to remember every detail and then go over it with her when she got home. "You're just hopeless, Lyndee," Angel sighed.

"A hopeless romantic, that's what I am. He's just so handsome! I can't believe you're not more excited."

"I'm happy to go out with my friend Langley and even happier to report every detail to you; how's that?"

"You don't have to be sarcastic, Angel. I've been on a couple of dates, and I just need to hear about yours for comparison. So be nice to your cousin, Lyndee." She smiled. Langley's knock at the door interrupted their friendly banter. Langley escorted Angel to his coach and they were off.

It was quiet sitting in the coach with Langley, with the only noise being the sound of the horses' hooves hitting the road in a slow trot. It made her uncomfortable at first, maybe because she hadn't seen him in a long time. She looked at him now. He had gotten taller with more width to his shoulders, and he no longer had a baby face.

In fact, he was quite handsome. She wondered why she had never been attracted to him. She made up her mind in the quiet of that moment. If all she wanted were looks and money, he would be her choice…but she was looking for love.

"What are you thinking, Angel? Are they thoughts you can share?" Langley asked, breaking the silence.

Angel was caught off-guard not knowing what to say, and then finally answering, "I was thinking we haven't seen each other in a long time. So how about letting me know what's been going on in your life." She finished with a breath of relief.

"Oh, I think what I've been doing would bore a young lady like you. Surely with all this education you're receiving, you must have much more interesting stories than I."

Angel couldn't help but be a little offended that he would think she wouldn't understand business matters. Papa had always included her in the daily paperwork of the ranch. Papa had insisted she know, and she was accountable to him.

She wondered now who took care of those duties. She put the

76

offense behind her and decided she would ignore any comments like that tonight. Breathing in deeply to calm herself, she relayed her story of how she had met Patrick and the work they were doing with the immigrants. Langley listened with polite interest. Her stories lasted until they pulled up to the theater.

Angel enjoyed the vaudeville performances. The bright costumes and sometimes garish make-up made the actors look a lot like clowns. Angel was shocked by some of the content but mostly entertained by the rest of the show.

The audience was made up of society's fames, as Aunt Lorraine would say. The women wore bustled dresses with veiled hats. The men wore top coats with tails and feathered hats, which they removed during the performances. Their dresses caused Angel to giggle more than once but only quietly to herself. As far as appearances, it looked as if the audience were in competition with the actors. Langley leaned his head closer to Angel's ear, "Are you enjoying the show?"

Angel caught her laughter; she didn't want Langley to think she was being disrespectful. "Oh quite, thank you so much for bringing me."

"It's always my pleasure to be an escort for a pretty young lady," Langley said, looking her over and appreciating her changes. "I do say that you've certainly blossomed into a beauty."

Angel blushed; she wasn't comfortable with that kind of attention from Langley, or conversely from anyone, "Once again, I say thank you. You've changed too, but then you were always good-looking." Angel felt as if she should return the compliment; then she changed the subject as the show closed to a loud round of applause. "Will you be leaving tomorrow?" she asked.

"Yes, in the afternoon. I happen to know a few of the actors from my father's outside investments. Would you like to go back stage and meet some of them, or should I be getting you home? I don't want your uncle to be mad at me or give him any cause to worry."

"Yes, I think I should get home; that would be best." Angel answered while Langley stood and took her by the arm. Angel put on her gloves, gathered her parasol and shawl, and then followed him

Edith Gleason

out to the foyer. They slowly made their way through the crowd. Spotting a clearing, they stepped out onto the oil lamp-lit streets of Boston. When his carriage arrived, Langley helped her up into the beautiful ornate coach. Once they were seated inside, Langley handed Angel the program from the show.

"I thought you might want to keep this as a souvenir to show your parents. Then they'll know you experienced some of Boston's finest culture while you were here. I wish I could stay longer and show you more of the city; but since Father died, all the responsibilities of the ranch and banking have fallen onto me. You'll have to visit me when you come back home. I'll show you some of the changes and improvements that I've made."

Langley scooted to the edge of his seat, then reached out and cupped her hands with his, as the carriage rolled to a stop. "Angel, if you asked me to stay here longer, I'd find a reason and a way to be here for you."

Angel was surprised; she hadn't expected this from Langley. "I'm sorry, but there would be no reason for you to extend your stay. Next week I'll be busy with college, and I won't have time for much else."

"You do understand what I'm telling you; I have strong feelings for you. I have the ways and means of making things happen for you, big things. Your life could be so much more interesting." Langley moved quickly and bent his head to kiss Angel; but she turned her head away from his advance, causing his kiss to fall on her cheek.

"Please, Langley. I don't feel that way about you. I appreciate the time you've spent with me, and I loved the stories from home; but I feel that I can only be your friend," Angel affirmed as she stopped and covered his hands with hers. "The Lord and I have already come to an agreement about where my life is headed. I really would like just to continue as friends."

"I don't need any more friends. I need a companion, a wife." Langley's eyes narrowed, "Don't pass on me so quickly, Angel. There may come a time you'll need someone of my standing and means. I may not be available then, and you'll regret the decision you're making now."

78

When Angel didn't reconsider, Langley withdrew his hands and scooted back in his seat. He sat stiffly and rigidly against it. "I won't be escorting you to the door. My driver will help you out. Good night, Angel." Langley didn't look at her again. He opened the door, and the driver helped Angel down the steps. She then closed the door on a deeply scorned Langley.

Angel was sorry her evening had to end that way. She never had any intention of hurting Langley. She tried to think of a way to soften his hurt, but in the end she knew that God would take care of it. This was a story which she would not tell to Papa or her brothers in detail because she knew that if she did, Langley's life wouldn't be worth spit. She would edit her story for her cousin Lyndee also. Langley had behaved as if his heart were broken; and Angel knew broken hearts were nothing to trifle with, nor did one want to.

Saddened by his refusal of her friendship, Angel walked slowly to the door. She would still regard him as a friend and continue to remember Langley in prayer.

Chapter Seventeen

The church service ended, so Lyndee and Angel made their way toward the door where the Reverend Reynolds waited to bid a good day to his parishioners.

Lyndee bent her head towards Angel and whispered, "When we get next to the Reverend, ask me how my mother's piano lessons are going."

"But your mother isn't taking piano lessons," Angel stated, a bit confused.

"Just ask me, okay?" Lyndee rushed her and Angel half-smiled in agreement. The Reverend Reynolds stood and shook Lyndee's hand. Lyndee gave a nod to Angel, and Angel knew that was her cue.

Angel begrudgingly obliged, "Lyndee, how are your mother's piano lessons going?" she asked, as sincerely as she could.

"I can't believe you just asked me that!" Lyndee exclaimed and burst into tears.

Aghast, Angel stuttered, "But I thought you …"

Lyndee interrupted her loudly, "You know my mother doesn't have any hands!" Then she continued bellowing. Angel was startled, then realizing it was a joke, burst into laughter; Aunt Lorraine had hands.

Angel had been set up once again by mischievous Lyndee. Both girls with their arms wrapped around each other, hurried out the door, and then they doubled over in tears of laughter. Unbeknownst to the Reverend that it was just a prank, he looked after them with sympathy and unbelievable disgust.

"Lyndee, you know I will never be able to show my face in that church again. I can't believe you did that to me!" Angel declared playfully, when the church was finally out of sight.

"You're going home next weekend anyway, so I wouldn't worry about it. Did you see the look on the Reverend's face? That was priceless. I'll never forget it."

"Oh Lyndee, you are such a clown. I think maybe that was a little mean to play on his emotions like that. I really don't know what to think of you sometimes. When you come to visit us in Montana, you're going to have to meet Casey. Even though I think you might be outmatched."

"It's a deal, little Angel; and just for you, I'll pen an 'I'm sorry' note to the Reverend for you and I. So don't worry about his feelings, okay? I'll be there in Montana before you know it; and you're going to miss me so much when you leave, you'll wish I was there with you, just like I'm going to miss you." Lyndee threw her arms around Angel and squeezed her so tight that Angel lost her breath for a moment.

Finally Angel was able to breathe again, "You know I'm going to miss you. You've been like a sister to me and made me feel so welcomed. Don't forget to write me whenever you can. I'll be thinking of you often, and when I do, I'm sure I'll be laughing."

"I'll be missing you too, cousin. And I know I'll be laughing along with my memories as well!" Lyndee said. Looking ahead, she spotted the house and changed the subject, "Race you." She took off on a run with Angel running not far behind her. While Angel ran to catch up, she thought that for Lyndee being a chubby girl, she sure could move. She beat Angel inside and was even able to snatch a cookie on her way up the stairs.

Angel stopped for a breather at the bottom of the stairs. For the life of her she couldn't understand how Lyndee hadn't caught a man yet. She made a mental note to tell Lyndee when it comes to men to slow down; it wasn't about a race. Angel giggled to herself, then ran up the stairs to laugh with her best friend and cousin, Lyndee.

*****

April was here in all of its spring glory. The daffodils had come into bloom; and the robins, along with the blue jays, were nesting and chirping their own songs to bring on the morning.

Aunt Lorraine made some oatmeal and was pouring it into several bowls for breakfast. Lyndee sat at the foot of the table with a grin on her lips that was fit for a Cheshire cat. Angel knew she was up to something on this April first, but she didn't have a clue what it was.

Uncle Jim was served first, and he scooped up plenty of sugar

81

into his hot cereal. Aunt Lorraine sat down at the table and did the same, while Angel and Lyndee followed this sweet tradition. Uncle Jim scooped up a large spoonful of oatmeal and promptly put it in his mouth. Almost as soon as he began to chew, he began to sputter and out came his oatmeal into his napkin. Aunt Lorraine and Angel followed suit, much to Lyndee's delight.

Angel now knew what Lyndee had been grinning about; she had replaced the sugar in the bowl with salt. Instead of a sweet tradition of an oatmeal breakfast, it had been turned into a salty April fool's concoction.

"What are we going to do with you, Lyndee?" Uncle Jim asked, not amused in the least. "I think you've got way too much time on your hands. This incident has helped me to decide that when Angel leaves for Montana, you're going to volunteer down at the shelter. I don't think it will hurt you to learn some appreciation for some of the things you take for granted."

"I'm sorry, Father, really. It was just an April fool's joke. I didn't mean any harm."

"That's just it, Lyndee; you never do. But you've wasted our breakfast, and food is not cheap. You'll have a chance to see how less fortunate people live and eat, and then maybe you will appreciate the simple things in life. You're a good girl, Lyndee, but you still need to learn and be taught a few life lessons."

Aunt Lorraine interjected as she rose from the table, gathering the bowls of wasted oatmeal. "Now this time you get to prepare breakfast."

Angel knew that Lyndee's punishment and her parents' loving correction stung. Angel felt Lyndee went too far. Angel knew that Lyndee felt bad, so she offered Lyndee help in making breakfast. She hoped it would help lessen the sting of her father's rectification.

Chapter Eighteen

"Cat, is my hearing failing me or do you hear that low rumble outside?" Hank asked his wife, taking his hat off and shaking the wet rain from his wraps as he quickly set the firewood down next to the fireplace.

"I don't hear it, but for some reason I do feel a rumble beneath my feet. What could that be?" Cat asked, concerned.

"The skies have looked overcast all day; it's blacker than I've ever seen it, and I noticed the leaves were turned up. It's been spitting rain, but nothing horrendous yet." Hank looked out the window, "Look at that the wind has kicked up. Look at them there windswirls, and yep, those dark clouds just released the rain. There were plenty of telltale signs it was going to be a big storm, so I had the ranch hands round up the cattle and put them in the barn. The boys already put away the farm equipment. Don't want it all rusting away on us."

"Do you think it will rain long? There is still snow in the mountains from the winter. It's been a mite cold and slow melt this season. That'd be an awful lot of water. I can't help to think that mightn't be good," Cat stated, looking troubled.

"What does God's word say about worry, Cat?" Hank gently reminded his wife.

"I know, I know; it says to 'be anxious for nothing.' It's just that a hard rain or a prolonged one wouldn't be good for the town or the people that built their homes on the sides of the mountains," Cat said but knew in her heart that God would take care of them.

The weather was always unpredictable, and she had seen the damage a storm could do. When she was little, she had watched as a tornado ripped her neighbor's ranch apart. Livestock and people flew through the air, and she observed them die as their bodies plummeted to the hard, unforgiving earth. She and her family had been spared, for which she was thankful. It was something she had witnessed and didn't want to see again. So yes, storms made her a little apprehensive, but she knew God forgave her for it.

Edith Gleason

For three long days the torrential rains persisted and pelted the Winters' ranch. Hank and Cat watched woefully as equipment and livestock washed out with the river of water that furled down the mountains. The waters rose higher and higher until it began to seep beneath the doors.

"Come on, Cat, we need to gather up what we can and take it upstairs." The wind howled and somewhere in the distance, there was a loud crack and a roaring that almost hurt their ears.

"Hurry, Cat, now just drop everything and run!" Hank grabbed Cat and hurriedly ran up the stairs, just in time to miss the breaking and splattering of the back kitchen windows with the burst of water not far behind. The rushing waters lapped at the steps behind them, filling the bottom floor to the middle of the stairs. With another loud cracking of the front windows, the waters flowed quickly down further towards town.

Reaching the top of the stairway, Cat screamed above the roar of the waters, "Hank, the children, where are the children?!" She was clutching the front of his shirt.

Hank covered her hands, "They're already upstairs. I told them to head there after they secured the barn." As soon as Hank had spoken, the children came out and gathered around their parents. They looked to Papa for reassurance.

"We need to pray, not just for us, but for the townsfolk too." Papa Hank bent his head, and in a loud voice he cried out to the Heavenly Father to rescue the people he knew and those he didn't. He prayed for salvation for those who would not see tomorrow.

The storm lasted for what seemed forever. The Winters family watched as some of their livestock washed down to the valley, along with some of their feed and grains for the coming winter. All they could do was continually offer up prayers to the Father in Heaven from which the rains came.

It had been five days of hard rain, and a weary Hank rolled over in bed and stretched. Something had awakened him. He lifted his head; it was the sunshine streaming through their bedroom window, accompanied by the song of a sparrow.

He nudged Cat, "Hey, sweetheart, the sun's shining. Maybe the storm is finally over." Hank stood up and walked over to the window, peering out at what looked like total devastation. His heart sank.

Carson came running in, "Papa, the rain has stopped!"

"Yes, I know, son; and it looks like we'll have work to do." Hank and Cat quickly donned their clothes. When they arrived downstairs, Toby and Tim were just coming into the kitchen.

"You boys already up and ready to go?" Hank asked.

"Yes, Sir, Papa," Tim answered.

Hank turned and kissed Cat on the cheek. "After we've checked out the ranch and barn, we'll be back for breakfast." Hank and the boys set out to inspect the damages from the storm, while Cat and Jeannette began cooking the morning meal before they started on the cleanup in the house. From Cat's past experiences, she knew it wouldn't be a pleasant task.

An hour later Hank and the boys entered the kitchen.

Toby spoke first, "We've lost about twenty head of cattle; and, from the looks of it, we lost all our winter feed for our animal stock. The fencing has all been torn up, and the barn needs some repair. Other than that, we're good to go." His report was grim.

Hank looked to Tim for the financial analysis. "I won't know about replacing the feed until we go to town and see what they have. As far as the cattle, we only lost a few. We don't have the finances to replace them; it's been a little snugger after using our profits from our sales last year to buy more cattle. We were counting on the profits from this sale to make it through the winter. Of course, there is the bright side: we won't have as much to feed, so we won't need as much grain. It's going to be tight, but I think we'll make it."

"After breakfast, we'll head to town to see what we can come up with. Bow your heads." Hank's prayer was somber as he and his boys sat down to the breakfast that Cat had prepared for them. They ate in silence, each one of them seeming to be in deep thought.

"What do you think we'll find when we get to town?" Toby asked, but everyone continued to eat in silence.

Hank drove the wagon with Tim and Toby sitting beside him. Cat helped load up the wagon with supplies and a lunch she thought

85

they might need. They had only traveled a short distance when the men were taken back by surprise as Papa noted how high the flood waters had been. He pointed out a water mark near the tops of trees.

"Papa, that mark has to be at least fifteen feet high, and look at all the trees it knocked down in its path." Toby was horrified.

"It was only by God's grace we were spared," Papa stated.

"Look over there, Papa, there has to be about ten boulders piled on top of each other. Almost as if someone picked them up and placed them there."

"Yes, nature did that. It's a powerful thing you just can't fight against something that's bigger than the lot of us. Do you see where the dirt is swirled around the rocks? That there must be the low part in the land, because that's where the boulders came to rest once the waters receded. Whoa!"

Papa suddenly called to the horses as he pulled the reins, bringing them to an instant stop, "Looks like the bridge is washed out too." He stood and looked at the land surrounding the water while he tried to remember where the shallow water lay. "We'll swing the team around and go up higher where the water is just a stream and cross there. It should be shallow enough by now."

Tim had sat in silence until now, "Papa, if the waters did this to the land, what do you think it did to the town?"

"We need to continue praying for them and do what we can once we get there. It's not going to be a pretty sight. Prepare your heart and your head."

The close family traveled the rest of the way in contemplative silence and prayer. It was dark by the time they reached town. Papa stopped the wagon, and the strong yet heavy-hearted men viewed the devastation that lay before them. There were only a few buildings left standing intact.

The mercantile, church and stables were demolished, along with the hotel. Bodies of animal life and some human remains lay lifeless across their path. Papa drove the team at a slow pace as quietly as he could so he could listen for any cries of help, but only a deathly silence echoed the horses' hooves. Finally putting down the reins and stopping the horses, they stepped down from the wagon. The boys and Papa rolled up their sleeves; there was work to do, and looking for survivors would be their first task. The dead would wait to be buried. It would be a sad and grim procedure, but this day one that had been born out of necessity.

Chapter Nineteen

"Help, help us please, someone!"

"Did you hear that, Papa? Sounds like a woman. Like maybe it came from over there behind the saloon." Toby pointed, holding up his lantern as he began walking briskly towards the cry for help.

Hank called after him, "We're right behind you, son."

When Hank and Tim reached Toby, he was already trying to administer aid to a bedraggled young woman. He was asking her questions.

"Where are you hurt? Is there anyone else you know of that needs assistance?"

"My arm is cut real bad, and it feels like my leg is broke. I tried to stand, but I just fell. I can't stand or walk," she answered, trying to stifle her tears. "Most of the townsfolk headed up to high ground when the mud slides came rushing down the mountain. My family was out in the fields trying to save what they could. My papa and mama tried to rustle together the family, but I hain't seen them. I think the mud's washed them all away." Then through her muffled sobs, "I just held on real tight to the saloon's sign until it broke loose, and I dropped down. I was too tired to hold on anymore." Then a glazed look came into her eyes as she realized she was alone, "My family, my family... they're all gone." Dropping her head in her hands, she continued to weep softly.

Hank turned to Tim, "Go get a blanket, some food and the bandages your mama prepared for us. You'll find them in the back of the wagon."

Tim hurried, but as he went, he was approached by some ranchers that had come to town to see if they could be of any help. "Sure glad to see you; I hope you came to help because we definitely could use a few extra pairs of hands," Tim greeted.

"We'll be glad to be of some assistance. We passed other people coming this way; they said they were coming to help so they should be here shortly. Hop down, boys; we got work to do," the man on the lead horse called out; and the men followed his orders. If there were

88

any other people who had survived, then time was of the essence.

*****

It was way into the early morning of the next day when the Sheriff stood amongst the men with a list that contained a body count and a total of burials that had to be done.

"It appears Amanda is the only survivor of the Bruffs' family. The rest of the list that I'm going to read are the survivors and people we've located: Grangers, the mercantile owners; Brenans, the saloon owners; Warners, the hotel keepers; McIvers, the stable tenders; and finally Miss Annabelle, the dress shop keeper. Anyone here that knows how to do doctoring will be welcomed over at the saloon; there's plenty that needs to be taken care of. Maybe some of you could provide a place to stay for these people until they get on their feet again. It's just temporary, mind you."

He cleared his throat and somberly read the list of the deceased. "The dead are as follows" – all around him the men removed their hats and bowed their heads in reverence – "the Mcandlas, family of four; the Jenners, family of five; the Hills, family of three; the Gustafsons, family of five; and finally the pastor Reverend Tom Wilkes. We've been working here for two days now; and I don't mean any disrespect, but we're tired and have our own families to get back to. So if you please, Hank, you wanna say a prayer for these here that have lost their lives. If you could do that, then we can start on their graves."

Hank nodded in agreement, then respectfully stepped up next to the Sheriff and politely asked everyone to bow their heads. Then he started, "Heavenly Father, we thank you for the rain that feeds our crops and livestock, not to mention ourselves. As you know, Lord, there are some that were overcome by the mighty efficient rains and the melting snows that came rushing down from your mighty mountains. There's not a name here you don't know; there's no person you don't recognize and no heart you can't heal. We ask that you welcome those we intend to bury. Wrap them in your arms and give them that warmth that they'll need, especially after this here long, cold rain. Your word says, 'Ashes to ashes and dust to dust,' so we give these people back that no longer have your breath of life into

89

the ground which you made us from. Lord, we ask for strength in doing our Christian duty for our lost brothers and sisters. In Jesus' name I ask it all, Amen."

The men set upon their weary tasks and labored until nightfall placing their friends in their final resting places. The women in the town sat up food provisions that had been gathered for the workers at the jailhouse, and all the men took turns eating. Each group ate with respectful silence out of sadness and pure exhaustion.

The Sheriff and town Constable had worked out a plan for helping to rebuild businesses that were ruined and families' homes that were destroyed. There was already news of materials and food that would be donated from nearby towns that hadn't been affected by the rains and had suffered little loss.

It was two days before the Winters' men made their slow journey home. They were tired and dirty, but oh so thankful that God had spared their own and their family's lives. Cat ran out to greet them and was surprised that they had brought Amanda Bruffs home with them.

Tim helped her down and into the house while Hank explained what had happened in town and that all of Amanda's family had been lost in the storm. Cat agreed that it was a good idea to give Amanda a place to stay; and with the Lord's help, they could always make room for one more.

Chapter Twenty

Miss Jessie had visited around Christmas time, and she brought along some sugary goodies from her newly opened candy shop. Since then, Angel has visited The Chocolate Petal many times, due to her aunt and uncle's requests for sweets. They weren't small people. Angel didn't mind, though; she had grown a taste for some of it herself.

Miss Jessie had hired on Lyndee and Angel for part-time work through the summer. Uncle Jim said it would keep them out of trouble. He was right; they were too busy to plan any other hijinks.

Lyndee excelled at the candy shop. She flitted busily around the customers and the candy. She even tried out some of her own recipes. Miss Jessica never had to look for Lyndee. She had found out early on that wherever there was loud laughter, there was Lyndee.

Lyndee loved the shop so much that she decided to stay on permanently after the summer was over. Miss Jessie was pleased with Lyndee's work and agreed to have her stay on. Being surrounded by all the food, candy, and people, Lyndee would definitely be in her element.

Angel, on the other hand, appreciated the work and the extra money it had brought her; but she was looking forward to going home. Teaching was her calling and she couldn't wait.

Late into every night after her Bible study, prayers and, of course, after her college studies were done, she could be found making plans to renovate the old schoolhouse. Since her arrival here, Angel had slowly been gathering books and school supplies with the extra money she earned at the candy shop. She was excited about her finds in this big city of Boston.

A lot of the reading materials she was able to acquire had been purchased at a bargain price. The Bostonians had already advanced beyond most of the materials Angel had bought, which is why she was able to secure such a bargain. Angel knew that the children in Montana would appreciate and relish them. It wasn't that Boston didn't appreciate education but that they were ahead of the children in Butte. Not for long, though, because Angel had plans to change it for the better for the children back in Montana.

It was June and graduation had finally arrived. Angel was sad that Patty wouldn't be here smiling up at her from the audience; she missed him. She was also saddened that Momma and Papa wouldn't be attending. They had written a letter of apology, saying that the crops and cattle needed tending to; and they couldn't afford to take the time off.

They had sent her a large check so she could get any supplies that might not be available in Butte. Angel would've traded the check and any monies for her parents to be there.

Graduation day had arrived, and Angel was dressed in her proper attire. She walked with the rest of her class to receive her diploma from the Dean. She had succeeded with top honors.

She was given a special award from Professor Jordan for her writing accomplishments; and, with a hug, he said, "I've enjoyed having you as a student in my class. I know you'll be successful in anything you attempt." His eyes actually teared up and so did Angel's. He was one of the people she had come to know well and respect; she would miss him.

Her aunt and uncle were proud of her and had rejoiced with her as if she were their own daughter. They were upset about her leaving but had accepted that one day she would have to leave. They would sorely miss her; and any time that she left would be considered too soon.

Lyndee planned a big going away party for Angel, and naturally Miss Jessie would be supplying the goodies. Angel had grown to love this family and her new friend, Miss Jessie. With a heavy heart she recounted times past that she had spent with them, and it would be with great sadness she would be leaving them behind in Boston.

Angel had almost all of her things packed for her trip back home, except for some souvenirs she had purchased for her family. She took those and placed them in her large quilted handbag for easy access. That way she could pass them out to each member when she saw them. She had to purchase another large trunk to carry the school supplies she had accumulated while she was there. She had just finished packing that trunk and was cleaning her room when Lyndee came in with a final letter from home.

Angel sat on her bed and began to read the letter from Momma,

My dearest Angel,

I write this letter with deep concern for our family's well-being. I'm sorry to inform you that the spring rains have washed away the old schoolhouse. Many of the townspeople have had to move away. A lot of their homes and land were demolished or damaged beyond repair. A lot of people lost their lives.

It was a hard spring, and Papa said he has never seen so much rain. Unfortunately we too lost some land. Now we don't have enough grazing land for the bison Papa purchased last year. We've had to let go some of the help. Papa is beside himself trying to figure out how to keep making a living.

Toby and Jeanette had their first baby and are now staying with us. All of your brothers are still at home. They've taken over a lot of the duties our former help did. They're good boys. We wouldn't have expected anything less. But it seems even with the extra hands gone, there is barely enough food and money to take care of what we have. Papa keeps saying that God will provide.

We are comforted in knowing that in God's word it says, "To everything there is a season, that we are perplexed on every side, cast down but not forgotten and finally that we are changed from glory to glory." We know that God is trying to teach us and we're trying to learn. Please pray for us.

On a final note, Langley stopped by with a proposal for your father. It concerns you, so Papa is thinking it over and wants to discuss it further with you when you get home. Toby and Jeanette want to meet you at the stagecoach when you arrive. I think they want to show off their little Adrian. Take care, Angel, and know you're in our prayers. We love you!

Love Always,
Momma, Papa, Toby & Jeanette,
Baby Adrian, Tim, Andrew and Carson Winters.

Edith Gleason

Angel sighed heavily. She hadn't been aware that things were so difficult back home. She had been so busy with her studies and job that, except for prayers, she hadn't given her family much thought. Angel put the letter on her bed, then knelt beside it.

Lyndee had been standing by; and after seeing how upset Angel was, she picked up the letter and scanned it. She knelt down next to Angel and put her chubby arm around her, then spoke softly, "God knows our need before we ask." Then they both began to pray.

Later on in the evening, Lyndee's party was a big success. Nellie and Miss Jessie and some of the people from school, as well as the students Angel had helped tutor, showed up for her big   send-off. Angel was forlorn, for she still looked for Patrick to show up and was disappointed when he didn't.

Nellie noticed her reticent look and gave her a reassuring hug, "Aye, me Wee Angel, he's with the Father." That caused Angel to smile, and she went about bantering with the rest of the guests.

Like all parties, there was too much food and too much noise; but it went down well with laughter and seemed to end too soon. Angel stood at the door and said goodnight to all of her guests, and with a hug and a thanks, she promised to pray for each one by name. Then she said goodbye; and, of course, all goodbyes are remembered and never forgotten.

Chapter Twenty-One

"Did you pack everything, Angel? Look through your bureau and make sure you didn't leave anything behind," Aunt Lorraine suggested as she was putting together a lunch for Angel's trip. Angel smiled. She was going to miss her aunt's businesslike ways and her genuine concern, always interested and eager to listen to anything you had to say.

"Yes, Aunt Lorraine, I've checked and rechecked; and I'm positive I have everything."

"Good, I wouldn't want to have to flag down a train. God forbid, I'd have to flex my muscles and pull it to a stop. I'm almost sure that's more than I could handle," Uncle Jim said with a wink. He was like Lyndee, always full of fun. In this family it was definitely true that the apple didn't fall far from the tree.

Angel chimed in, "Yes, Uncle Jim, I couldn't bear to see you stop a moving locomotive." She smiled and Uncle Jim returned it.

"Hey, little cousin, don't leave me out of this. I'd run after you too. Just hold a piece of candy in front of me, and I'll follow you to the ends of the earth," Lyndee teased and lovingly put her arms around Angel's shoulders. She gently put her face against Angel's cheek.

Angel returned her hug. "I've enjoyed my stay here, and I appreciate you letting me stay. You just don't know how much I'm going to miss all of you."

They all began to tear up when Uncle Jim shouted, "Group hug!" That was the cue for all of them to gather around with Angel in the middle this time and squeeze for all they were worth. Angel survived; she always did.

After wiping their eyes and straightening themselves, Aunt Lorraine commanded, "Off to the train with you. You've got a long journey ahead of you." Then, pulling Angel close, she whispered, "We'll be praying for all of you. Here is a little something to give your parents from us." Aunt Lorraine slipped a folded check into her hand. "I'm going to miss you, my only adopted child." Then Aunt

95

Lorraine promptly kissed her cheek. "You let us know if you ever need anything, and don't be afraid to holler 'cause I'll hear ya."

"I won't be afraid to holler. All of you write me and let me know how you're doing, and don't forget to let me know how Lyndee's career is taking off too." Angel rubbed her belly, leaving Lyndee in giggles.

"You be ready for me, little cousin, 'cause I'm comin' out there," Lyndee promised.

Uncle Jim helped Angel aboard the train; then the family she had grown to love stood together at the station. Looking out the window, she smiled and waved until her family was out of sight.

Sadly she whispered her last goodbye. After wiping her eyes, she gave a final wave. She offered up a prayer of safety and prosperity for her makeshift family from Boston. She then thanked the Lord for all that he had brought into her life; she felt she was a better person because of it.

Settling back in her seat, she reached inside her bag and found her Irish locket that Nellie had dropped off to her. She said she found it amongst Patty's belongings with a note to give to Angel as a graduation gift. Angel smiled as she caressed it and traced it with her fingers. She carefully unfolded the handwritten note that Patrick included with her gift and, for the first time since she had received it, began to read it.

My Dearest friend Angel,

I give this cross pendant as a promise to you that I will accept your Lord Jesus one day soon. I thank you for caring enough about me to want to include me in your heavenly home. As us Irish would say, 'May the rains sweep gentle across your fields, may the sun warm the land, may every good seed you have planted bear fruit, and late summer find you standing in fields of plenty.

Your friend, Patrick

Angel sighed and looked out her window. She could have sworn she saw Patrick's face in the clouds; but, when she looked again, it was gone as quickly as it had come. Angel whispered a prayer,

96

"Thank you, Lord; I know you're taking care of him and thank you for letting me see him one last time. It was a comfort to me. Amen."

She placed the cross around her neck; but, before closing her bag, she withdrew her journal and pencil and began to put her thoughts on paper. Angel was interrupted by a small voice that whispered her name. She looked up at the doorway only to see a towheaded boy with curly locks. His bright eyes caught her attention. Then he giggled and, in a swirl of white, swiftly ran away.

Angel smiled and cooed, "Zachery." She looked down again and penned her thoughts.

Dear Diary,

I'm headed home to Montana with a teaching degree in my hand and a hurt in my heart. It seems my return has a guise about it, and I don't know what it is. I'm leaving it in the Lord's hands. I'm confident he'll take care of it.

However, I keep seeing and dreaming about my little brother Zachery. He's always trying to tell me something or warn me. I know with all my heart he is in heaven, but I think the Lord has him running about to tell me something of importance. I miss him so much that it still hurts. I'm counting on you, Heavenly Father, to make me strong.

Angel put her things away, then rested her head against the window and quickly nodded off. The train rocked her head back and forth, and her dream began.

*****

The winds were kicking up; the dust storms were whirling and huge. She ran, but objects of all sizes and shapes came at her from every angle. She fell and tried to claw at the grass, but only clumps would pull up out of the ground and left her to weep in despair. She looked up, her face muddied and streaked from her tears mixed with mud. She blinked to clear her vision, and she could plainly see an outline of a boy.

"Zach! Zach, is that you?" she called. "Why do you haunt me,

97

baby? I said I was sorry. Do you want me to die too? Zach, don't leave me! Please, come back!" She screamed as the boy turned and began to run away. She clawed at the air and tried to move toward him, but she was frozen to the ground. Wiping her face, she looked again and the boy was gone.

A voice so loud it hurt her ears screamed, "There is no redemption in life!" Angel dropped her head back into the mud and cried her heart out.

Exhausted, she began to disappear. It was as if every teardrop she shed had become a piece of her that was falling away. Coughing and trying to catch her breath, she sobbed into the wind until there were no visible pieces left of her. In the place she had just been, there was now only a small voice lamenting over and over, "I'm sorry. I'm sorry."

Drained and feeling hopeless, Angel looked around and found that she lay quietly in a set of angelic hands, so soft and so strong. A commanding voice spoke aloud, "I've got you. I've held you in my hands since the day you were born. Did you really think I would leave you? That was the world and yourself holding you responsible for something you had no control over. Stop crying now and lift up your head. Redemption has always been a prayer away. It's always been found in forgiveness. Sometimes you have to forgive yourself before you can forgive others."

Then he whispered ever so tenderly, "I have always and will always love you, and I promised before your world began that I would never leave you." He set Angel down on solid ground, where there were neither storms nor troubles of her own making, just peace and quiet and love.

A soft breeze touched Angel's face, causing her to wake up. A wisp of her hair gently lifted against her cheek, then fell to her shoulders. She looked around. The window was closed, and there were no other passengers in her car. A small voice sweetly whispered in her ear, "You so pretty, Ainjo." And then all was quiet. Angel stared ahead as her eyes filled with tears and dripped to her chin. "I love you too, Zachery." Then she looked down at her thumb-clenched fists.

*****

The train rides and the ferry were just as beautiful as the first time Angel had seen them, yet this time they seemed like a blur. The long journey and the lengthy time it lasted gave her time to assess her situation at home and to think about Casey. The foremost thoughts in her mind were her family back home and how devastated they must be due to their suffering caused by the rains. Angel's every waking moment, even her dreams, were shrouded by her prayers for her family and friends.

The next transfer to the stagecoach now entering Montana was her last. Once again everything began to look familiar to Angel. Her heart began to beat a little faster as she became excited for this ride to end, for home was just ahead.

Angel started to feel nauseous. She could only guess it was from the anticipation she felt from not knowing exactly what sort of dilemma and what problems her family were now facing. She calmed herself down the only way she knew how, by repeating the verse, "I have learned whatever state that I am in therewith to be content and to be anxious for nothing."

Feeling calmer, she leaned against her seat. She whispered a prayer of thanks to the Lord for his comfort and then left all of her cares in his hands. Enclosed safely in the Lord's arms, she closed her eyes and napped the rest of the way to Butte, Montana.

Chapter Twenty-Two

Angel peered out her window as the stagecoach pulled into Butte. There, standing on the walkway just as Mama had promised, stood Toby, Jeanette and baby Adrian (who by now was at least a year old). Toby was wrestling with his squirming son, yet had the biggest smile on his face that could only belong to a proud new papa.

Angel stepped down with the help of the coach driver. Tears were streaming down her face as she ran to her big brother and jumped into his embrace. Jeannette stepped over and hugged her too. Inside Angel's memory she could hear Uncle Jim's words calling out, "Group hug!" With Toby's release, her feet touched the ground. Looking around, Angel knew that she was finally home.

During the ride home, Angel looked at the devastation that the rains had left behind. They passed the old red schoolhouse; but all that was left of the building were splintered boards, along with desks and broken chairs scattered about the yard. There was nothing left that remotely resembled the school she knew.

Angel felt a stab in her heart and a sickness in the pit of her stomach. She felt as if her dream had been crushed. "Why? Why would God allow such devastation to the very people that serve him? Did we not do as he asked, or did we not do enough? Did he stop loving us?"

Toby placed his arm around Angel. "It's not what we do that makes the Lord take care of us or love us. The Bible says that he rains on the just and unjust alike. If God kept us from every foe or harm, no one would ever need faith. He wants us to trust in him and cast our every care upon him. Though we don't see him, we love him for who he is and for sending his son to die for us. The sinner dies and so does the Christian. And God is the God of all."

"I know that; I'm just in shock. Thank you for reminding me. It's just that when I saw this, I was overcome. I know the Lord takes care of us. Even through this, we as Christians are examples to the unsaved, so that through this, they can see that God takes care of his children. That's why I know in my heart Momma and Papa are going to be okay." Angel felt a peace that for a moment she had almost forgotten.

"That's right and so will you, Angel. A building can be rebuilt; lives can be changed. God will provide," Toby finished.

Angel looked at her brother through tear-filled eyes with a newfound feeling of respect and smiled, "If I didn't know better, I'd think I was sitting next to Papa. You've grown so much. I've missed you, big brother." Angel wrapped her arms around him again and squeezed, while Toby melted in her embrace. Little sister had come home and she was all grown up.

"Look who's here, Papa!" Cat threw her dish towel on the counter and grabbed onto Angel. "Our little Angel, oh we've missed you so much! And look how you've grown!" Momma was hugging and twirling Angel while she was exclaiming.

Papa had entered the room at Momma's squeal. He hurried over and held both women in his arms. "My little girl, my little girl!" was all he could say as they hugged and danced in the middle of the room.

Toby, Jeanette and Adrian stood back and let Tim, Andrew and Carson get their hello hugs in too. They all rejoiced for a good while, then Mama excused herself and went back to making dinner.

"I guess I should take my things upstairs and unpack. I think I'm going to lie down for a while. It's been a long trip and I'm tired, unless you need my help, Momma," Angel offered.

"No, baby, you go on up and get some rest. The boys will carry up your bags and trunks. You can help later after you've rested and settled back in. It's good to have you home."

Cat smiled and went back to her cooking while the boys helped with Angel's things. Papa stood in the background and appeared anxious about something. For what, Angel didn't know; but if she knew her father, she would soon find out.

Chapter Twenty-Three

Papa sat at his desk going over the bills and figuring out the next month's budget. He was intense and his brows were furrowed. Toby was seated across from him; he was the numbers expert, which was one of the reasons he and his family had stayed on to continue helping his Papa with the family business.

"I don't think you should agree to Langley's proposal, Papa. There must be another way. I think we just need to pray about it some more," Toby said quietly.

"You don't think that I haven't prayed about it? I've prayed so hard that my tears and sweat were so mingled, you couldn't tell which was which. I don't like the idea either, but I have no other recourse. God in his infinite wisdom knows what we are going through. If he wants to stop it, he will." Papa was angry, but not at Toby. He was mad at himself and, yes, a little upset with God. That he should even have to consider such a proposal was preposterous.

Angel had approached Papa's office and heard the anger in his voice. Her brother Tim had told her when she awoke that Papa wanted to talk to her in his office. She knew it was something serious but didn't know what it was about. When she heard him talking, she stopped and prayed that God would guide her and her papa in whatever was to be discussed or in any decision that was to be made.

Papa looked up when he heard the swish of petticoats against the door. "Angel, come in. I was expecting you. How did you sleep?"

"I slept well, Papa; but, in fact, I'm still tired."

"Sleep is one thing you can never really catch up on. Once it's gone, it's lost. Your body will just require more rest for the next week or so, but you'll recover and be fine. Please sit down, sweetheart."

Angel moved to sit next to her brother; but as soon as she sat, Toby rose and excused himself, saying he had chores to attend to. He said he would see them later at dinner time.

"What is going on, Papa? I heard your voice when I was approaching the door, and there was anger in it. Did I do something to make you angry?"

After the Rains

"No, Angel. It's just that I don't like what we have to talk about, and I wish there was a different answer."

"Papa, please tell me whatever it is; and, if it is that undesirable, we can work it out together. I know you would never do anything purposely to harm anyone, especially me; and I trust that you will make the right decision."

"If only it were that easy. Angel, as you know, we lost a large section of our grazing land for the bison and cattle, due to the horrendous amount of rains we experienced this spring. Our ranch is surrounded by Langley's land. I offered to purchase some of his property, which would include payments, of course; but he wouldn't hear of it. Instead, he suggested another proposal. In exchange for land, he wants your hand in marriage." Papa sighed heavily, closed his eyes, and threw his head back against his chair.

That's what all this was about? Angel was dumbfounded. Why would Papa do this? "Did you agree, Papa?"

"I'm sorry to say that I did. I told him you would date him exclusively for the next three months; and during that time if we happened upon a better solution, it was no longer a deal."

"Did you think about or even consider my feelings in this matter, Papa? That I might not want nor will ever agree to marry Langley?" Angel was enraged, but it was a righteous anger.

"I've done nothing else but think of you. I've prayed about it; and I've considered not just your future, but the future of your momma, your brothers and the ranch hands we support. Angel, at this time, there is more at stake here than just your happiness."

"Are you punishing me for what happened to Zach? Have you still not forgiven me?" Angel felt a pang in her stomach.

"This has nothing to do with what happened to Zach. I won't discuss that with you. This is a different matter altogether," Papa said through tight lips.

Dismissing the raw hurt she felt inside, she decided to fight back. Curling her hands into tight fists with her thumbs poking out between her forefingers and middle fingers, she ranted, "I'll fight it, Papa. I love you, but Langley is not the one I'm meant to spend the rest of my life with. I just know it; he's not the one."

103

Edith Gleason

"Angel, you have no say in this matter. Women have no rights. You can't own land or even vote. Out of love and out of your duty to the family, you'll do as I say. If you want a different solution, then just keep praying for another way out of this mess."

"Papa, is that why you wanted me home? Am I your ticket to financial freedom? Where is your faith?" Angel stood and turned to leave, then turned back to face her father, "I'll do as you say, but I won't make it easy for you or anyone else involved in this matter. Are we through here? I have a school curriculum to construct and figure out where to hold school."

Angel felt betrayed and dejected. She wasn't sure what she was supposed to do now. She didn't even know if she should follow through on her education and make the school situation happen. Papa was sad. He agreed with Angel; she shouldn't have to marry anyone she didn't choose. But circumstances at this time dictated her future, unless God intervened.

"Langley will be over this evening after dinner; please be ready. Now we are through here." Papa looked down and rifled through his paperwork again, as if the answer he had been looking for could be found amongst the papers. Angel stepped back and watched Father with a feeling of empathy. Here was a man that, for the first time in his life, had to agree to one of the hardest thing he'd ever done.

Angel offered softly, "Your answer is not in the papers, Papa; it's in prayer. If you'll excuse me, I'm sure my services are needed in the kitchen." She turned to go, then stopped and turned around at the door and spoke, softly addressing her father once more, "No matter what comes our way, I still and always will, love you, Papa." She went over and kissed her father on his forehead, then hurried out of the office, leaving a broken man with tears streaming down his face, uttering another prayer of, "Please, God."

Angel stood outside the door, listening to the sobs of her father. Clutching her hand to her heart, she repeated a verse, "Thou art my hiding place; thou shalt preserve me from trouble; thou shalt compass me about with songs of deliverance. Selah."

104

Chapter Twenty-Four

Carson slowly snuck up behind Angel in the dining room and bellowed, "Boo!" He laughed as Angel jumped, almost knocking her little brother to the floor. "Did I scare you? I know I did."

"Carson, is there another reason for your presence in this room, I mean besides trying to scare the living daylights out of me?"

Carson was holding his sides and trying to get his giggling under control. He straightened, "Yeah, Tim and I wanted to take you over to the old schoolhouse area and see what needs to be done. So we can start to rebuild it."

Angel was overcome with joy, "What? You would do that for me?"

"Yeah, you're our sister, anything for family." And then with a tease in his voice, "I heard Casey's s'posed to be back today, and Tim said he might be there too."

Angel caught her breath and all of a sudden was in a hurry, "Let me get my wrap and I'll meet you out front."

"Boy, I ain't ever seen you jump like that before. Maybe I should drop Casey's name more often, like when I want dinner." Angel knew Carson was only teasing, so she didn't lecture him. Instead she laughed; he was the baby of the family, and he took full advantage of it.

Tim brought the wagon to a stop and pulled on the brake to keep the wagon from rolling downhill. He hopped down and lifted Angel to the ground.

"Hey, where's my lift?" Carson demanded.

"Uh, kid, you're on your own. You can do it; I have faith in you. Just put one foot in front of the other and jump," Tim answered him back.

"Oh I see. Angel's the only one that gets special treatment. Okay." Carson was done trying to get a lift so he scrambled down out of the wagon. Angel was already walking around and surveying the grounds.

"Tim, we'll have to start from scratch. It appears there may be nothing salvageable," Angel spoke with dismay.

"No problem," Tim said, coming to stand next to her. "The other towns have promised to donate any materials our town needs to help us rebuild. Your schoolhouse was on that list."

"Oh, Tim, God is good." She clasped her hands together.

"Yes he is, Angel. I brought my writing pad along, so we can figure out to a near penny or a close estimate of what we'll need. I think I found a couple of desks that can still be used and some chairs that can be put back together. It will take some elbow grease and lots of time, but we can do it."

"It will go quicker, especially with a few extra hands." A voice that Angel recognized as Casey's came from behind them. Angel and Tim turned to see Carson wearing a wide grin and holding onto a tall, older, and more filled-out Casey. Angel ran to her old friend and threw her arms around him.

Laughing the whole time, Casey picked her up in a twirl while hugging her at the same time, "I've missed you, Angel."

"Oh, Casey, you don't know how much I've missed you." Casey sat her down and couldn't help looking her over.

"You're beautiful, Angel. Boston has been good to you," he remarked with a twinkle in his eyes.

"It was good to me, but it is better to be home. And you, Casey, how have you been?" She beamed.

"I have been just fine. Like you, though, a little surprised at how things were going here. It's sad, but I can still see potential. I've come back with a preacher's license. Unfortunately, the church is another building that needs to be, if you pardon my pun, resurrected," he said regretfully.

"That's not all I've heard you have. How is Rachael?" Angel wasn't sure why, but just now her heart hurt.

Tim interrupted, "The fund that the town has for rebuilding has already included the church. All of the townspeople will have to pitch in and help one another out. With time and a little hard work, it can be done." He was the only one of Angel's brothers that always leaned toward optimism. This time it appeared he had good reason.

Casey's eyes were sad as he turned away from Angel, "Yes, I

heard about that, and I am very thankful. I'd rather we help the people with their needs first. A church is a body of people, not a building. We can hold services out on the lawn for now. 'All good things come to he who waits.'" Casey smiled.

"You sound like a preacher, Casey. Boy, living in this town with you as a pastor and Angel as a teacher is going to take some getting used to. Congratulations, pastor Casey." Tim reached out and shook Casey's hand. Angel guessed from the way Casey avoided her question that now was not the time to discuss Rachael, so she didn't broach the subject again. She was sure Casey would tell her in his own time.

"Yes, Casey, congratulations are in order. Why don't you and your father come to dinner tonight, and we can discuss what kind of work actually lies ahead of us?" Angel suggested.

"That sounds like a good idea. Count us in. Is there anything you'd like us to bring?" Casey asked.

"Just bring yourselves, Brother Casey," Tim said, slapping Casey on the back. "I'm right proud of you, boy. You did well for yourself. I think we're done here for now; we just came out here to give it a look-see. We'll talk more tonight at dinner. Right now we need to get back so Carson here can finish his chores," he said with a tease.

"What chores? I finished everything Papa gave me," Carson whined.

"Well, you haven't even touched any of the things I'm thinking of."

"Tim, you're just funning with me. I'll race you to the wagon." And off Carson ran.

"That kid is wising up to me. I think I'm going to have to teach him a lesson." Turning on his heels in pursuit of his little brother, Tim yelled, "The tickle monster is coming and he's coming for you, Carson."

Angel looked after her brothers and laughed, "You'd think they'd get tired of that game; but it seems the older they get, the worse they get."

Casey's look softened as he looked at Angel. "The word is that you're dating Langley. Out of all the people in this town, I wouldn't

Edith Gleason

have ever guessed Langley was your type."

"I am and he's not," Angel answered curtly.

"Well, Angel, try not to put too much information in your answers. I wouldn't want to try to figure out what you're talking about," he said with a hint of sarcasm.

"I'm sorry, Casey. Langley is a sore spot for me. Yes, I've seen him a couple of times in the past two weeks. I wouldn't think it was anything serious, but my papa does. It seems he's promised my hand in marriage to Langley in exchange for land, unless something else happens." Angel turned to go to the wagon, but Casey reached out and held onto her arm.

"I refuse to believe that. Hank would never do that."

"Believe it, Casey. Papa wasn't trying to punish me, though. I understand that he was just thinking about the other people that get taken care of because of this ranch."

"I'll talk to him, Angel. Maybe there is something else he hasn't thought of yet," Casey said sincerely.

"You can if you want to, but Papa's mind is made up. There is nothing anyone can do, except pray." Angel looked down.

"That's the best tool we have, so I'll do that. Let me walk you to the wagon and help you up. I see your brothers have finally calmed down, and I wouldn't want to stir them up and get them started all over again," Casey teased.

Angel and Casey were quiet the rest of the way. But it didn't stop Casey from contemplating the situation and the possibility of another solution. He was sure there was one and that God in his time would reveal it.

Chapter Twenty-Five

The laughter and loud talk around the dinner table was especially festive this early fall evening. Dessert was being served when a knock sounded on the door. Andrew rose to answer the door and led in Langley. As soon as his eyes caught sight of Casey, his face turned sour.

"I didn't know you were back. It seems pastors' degrees don't take as long as other degrees to secure," Langley said curtly with a smug smile. "However, it is nice to see you, Casey." Casey stood and shook Langley's hand.

"Thank you. It's nice to see you too. I like doing my heavenly father's business. How about you? I hear they keep you busy doing your father's business. I was sorry to hear about your father's passing; I pray you're doing well," Casey said, sitting back down to momma Cat's apple pie.

"Thank you, I am doing quite well. Yes, my father was taken out of this world too soon. He could turn everything he touched into gold; he was a great businessman. What he left me was a great legacy for making money. Of course I will miss him, but I don't need sympathy. Us Williamses always snap back in the face of adversities."

The table talk fell silent. Langley looked around the table and spotted Angel. "Angel," he tipped his hat and nodded, "I'd like to speak to you, if I may?"

Angel stood, picking up her plate. "Yes, in the parlor if that's okay? Just let me take care of the dinner dishes first. Would you like a piece of Momma's pie?"

"Yes, that sounds good. A man in his right mind would never refuse any of Cat's homemade pies. I'll just take it in the parlor, if you don't mind. Go ahead and finish what you're doing, and I'll be waiting."

Angel and Cat began to collect the dinner dishes when Cat spoke, "The ladies in town are starting a quilting bee. They want to have enough quilts in store so that every family has a warm blanket to at least keep them through the winter. After a flood like that, the winters here in Montana are brutally bitter and cold. Do you want to lend a hand in the bee, Angel? Or do you think your time will be all tied up with your schooling?"

Angel turned her attention towards Momma, "A quilting bee? Will we be making quilts for the flood victims?"

"That is the women's intentions, I believe," Cat answered.

"That sounds great, Momma. Yes, I'll make time. It will be good to help other people out." Angel and Cat finished cleaning up the table as the men continued their talk.

"We went over to the old schoolhouse today, Papa. It looks like some of the materials are still useful. Toby and I are going to write a list of supplies that we'll need to rebuild some of the furniture for the school," Tim stated, while shoving his last bite of pie into his mouth.

Langley stopped dead in his tracks, his pride stinging from the words he had just heard. He turned around to address the dinner group. "If you're talking about the school on the hill, you needn't bother. Once Angel and I are married, she won't be working. No Williams' woman works outside of the home. Besides, that should save you extra work. On whether or not she wants to quilt, well, that's entirely up to her."

Papa looked up from his plate, "We will be building the school. It will be Angel's decision as to whether or not she will be teaching for at least the first year. She could train an understudy to teach after she is gone; that is, if that is what she wants. You won't have any children, at least right away, so I would think you would want her to have something productive to do with her time," Hank replied a bit snidely.

"I guess the matter is really between husband and wife, but I thank you for your concern, sir." Langley gave Hank a polite nod and then headed to the parlor. The family finished their dessert in silence. Papa devoured his pie with more fervor than he needed. He was angry; yet in his thoughts, he continued with silent prayers and finished each one with, "Only you, Lord, know better than I."

The family settled in the sitting room, giving Papa the lead in conversation, "I'll be going to the livestock sale over in Virginia

110

City. They have the best prices. I'll be taking Toby and Tim, so you two, Andrew and Carson, need to take over their ranch duties. I'm sure you'll be able to handle it. Wes and Billy said they would come over and give us a hand if we needed it. I'll let them know."

"About how long will you be gone, sir? I'll have some extra time on my hands for now, so I can help too," Casey offered.

"That would be fine, young man. You were always a good worker, outside of your pranks, that is," Hank smiled.

"I didn't know you were aware of those, sir," Casey said, slightly embarrassed.

"There isn't much that goes on here that I don't know about, son. You were always a good friend to my Angel, and I know you'll continue to be one. I thank you for that. Your daddy did a good job raising you; you turned out well. I, for one, am proud to know you." Hank stood and shook Casey's hand. "Welcome home, Casey. It's good to have you back."

Casey, feeling a bit emotional, replied, "Thank you, sir; it's good to be back. I want you to know that I'm praying about this plan for Langley and Angel. I believe God will give us another answer, if we give him enough time and listen."

Papa grinned, "I was counting on that, son." The family was all in agreement that Papa and his boys would be gone about two weeks. They then sat about, discussing their plans for rebuilding the town.

In the parlor, agreement was not the subject. Angel was fuming, "What do you mean I won't be teaching? Who do you think you are?"

"I don't want to argue about it. But, after all, you are just a woman."

"We're not married yet; and, if I were you, I wouldn't count on it. Langley, how can you want me when you know I don't love you?" Angel sat down and her tone was softer.

"Since when did marriage have anything to with love? They've always been about arrangements. That's all that is going on here," protested Langley.

"That makes me sad to think you have no other expectations from marriage except for financial gain. My momma and papa love

111

each other; so do Toby and Jeanette, and they chose one another. Don't you want more for yourself? Don't you think you deserve more? I know I do."

"That's one of the differences I see between you and I; every decision in life, for me, is more like a business decision. The better the deal, the more you get out of it." Langley pulled Angel close to his side and then lowered his lips to her face.

Angel put her hands up and tried to push him away. "No Langley, I won't! I won't let you!"

"I believe Miss Angel said 'No.' I'm sure that you, being the gentleman you are, would regard her feelings." Casey stood at the door, his hands curled into fists. Langley released Angel, and she quickly stood up and moved away from him.

"I respect anyone who respects me." Langley rose and straightened his attire. "Miss Angel, it's been a pleasure. I'll be seeing you later, and we'll work on that kiss." He smiled smugly and walked briskly past Casey.

"Casey." And with a quick nod he was out the door.

"That guy has never changed. He has everything and yet he still demands more. Are you okay, Angel?" Casey came to her side.

"Yes I am, thanks to you. You know, I don't hate Langley; I just feel really sorry for him. He's always gotten everything he's wanted in life, except for love." Angel put her head against Casey's arm and sighed.

"Yeah, well, don't feel too sorry for him. You're next on his list of wants." Casey put his arm around her shoulders and escorted her to the main room.

"Yes, I know what he wants, but what he and God want are two different things. Don't tell Papa what happened with him, please. I don't want to upset him any more than he is. I can handle Langley; I just give him to the Lord," Angel was pleading.

"All right, but if he does that again, you let me know; and I'll be the one to help the Lord take care of him," Casey promised.

Angel looked up at him before they entered the room, "Thank you, Casey, I will. Did I tell you how much I've missed you?" Angel's words lit Casey's face up with a smile as he entered the room.

112

Both of them paused as Casey asked, "Did I tell you how much I enjoyed your letters and being included in your journey? If I haven't yet, then I thank you." Angel smiled and, reaching over, squeezed his hand and beamed while she led him into the room to join her family in their ongoing discussion.

Chapter Twenty-Six

The town's construction team had almost finished building a good portion of the people's houses that had been destroyed and were now working on the schoolhouse. Most days Angel rode her horse to the site, and today was no different. It was drier than normal, so each gallop of her horse's hooves stirred up more dust. Angel had had enough of choking through the dust, so she decided to dismount and walk her horse the rest of the way.

"Where are you walking to, Miss Angel, and on such a pretty day, all by yourself?" Wes had ridden up beside her.

Angel, being surprised, turned around to greet him, "Where have you been hiding? I haven't seen hide nor hair of you since I got back."

"Oh, I've been around, mostly hanging out at Margareet's; I've been helping to break and train her father's horses. I heard around town that you had finally come home. I'm glad you're back; personally speaking, the place wasn't the same without you." He smiled, looking down at her. "When you going to come out to the races again? I miss that pretty face of yours, sneaking a look over at me." A strange unfamiliar whiff passed her nose; and, because of the rumors that were around, she could only guess it was alcohol.

"You know, I was a lot younger then. I don't want to burst your bubble, but my taste in men has changed. Don't get me wrong; you're still pretty to look at, just not my type," Angel teased.

"Really, and is Langley? I don't think his money will let him appreciate how pretty you've grown. You're right easy on the eyes, Miss Angel." Wes hadn't missed how beautiful she had grown. He had always known that she would be a beauty, but not like this. All of a sudden, something inside him wanted her. It wasn't the booze talking; it was sheer lust.

"So you know about Langley too. Is nothing private anymore?" Angel asked, dismayed.

"Only the things that don't matter are private. Where are you headed?" Wes asked with interest.

"I'm going to the schoolhouse to see if I can help out. Why don't you come along? I'm sure they could use you, and extra hands always make less work." Angel knew they could use all the help they could get, and Wes had always been a hard worker.

"I think that I will. All my chores are done for now and, besides, I'll get to spend more time with you."

"Wes, I thought you were engaged?" Angel asked, trying to remind him of his commitment.

"Nothing is written in stone yet. I'm still free to look. Do you still want my help?"

"I'm sure they will." Angel stopped and swung up onto her horse, "I'm tired of walking." She galloped alongside Wes to their destination. Their conversation had fallen silent when she turned to him and asked, "Do you want to race?" Without any further prodding, off they raced.

When they arrived at the school, Angel triumphantly hopped down from her horse, then, after the dust had settled, declared herself the winner. A disgruntled Wes brushed sand and dirt from his clothes. The workers were glad to see them and even happier with one more pair of hands to help them with their work.

"Here," Angel giggled as she handed Wes a hammer, "Second prize."

Wes grinned, "I couldn't have asked for more, thank you." The workers were glad for Wes's help. He worked hard while he was there; but it seemed that every time Angel turned around, there he was. Not to mention that Casey never seemed too far behind. She didn't know how he did it.

It flustered her somewhat to think that she had never really given Wes a second thought while she was in Boston, but now here he was and all but seeking her attention. Angel felt flattered, yet she wasn't sure what to do about his attention. Given time, she was sure she'd figure it out.

Then there was Casey, always smiling and eager to help others. He had grown into such a handsome young man. More charming than any man she had ever met. Angel was sure he was going to be a great catch some day for some lucky young woman like Rachael; she was just sorry it wouldn't be her.

115

Edith Gleason

The sun was lowering in the big country sky, and it was time to clean up and head home to dinner. Everyone was tuckered out and dragging, but they were determined to make it home. Right now hunger was more important than sleep. Casey said his goodbyes and headed back to town. Angel watched him leave; she couldn't help feeling proud of what he had become.

"Billy and I will be coming over to your ranch while your Pa and your brothers go to Virginia City. Hank asked us if we would help when they were gone, and we said, 'yes.' Maybe, if Langley lets you, we can do some riding while I'm there. They're leaving tomorrow, aren't they?" Wes asked, tightening the straps on his saddle and watching the direction of Angel's eyes as she watched Casey ride off.

Angel had already mounted her horse. "Yes, that's the plan. I'm sure my papa will appreciate your help while he's gone. Why don't you stop over for dinner and you can tell him yourself? That'll make him feel more at ease about leaving. As far as Langley letting me ride, he doesn't own me; and, besides, I don't think you could keep up with me."

Wes swung up, "I'll do that." He looked at her with a challenge in his eyes, "Can't keep up, huh? Let's just see if you can keep up with me. Race you?"

Angel didn't need any excuse; she had missed riding her horse, and any opportunity to race him was welcomed. Both of them nudged their horses and were off, racing toward the ranch. Langley was waiting at the ranch. He had taken a seat on the front porch swing. He scowled when he recognized Wes as the other rider coming in with Angel. He rose and walked to the edge of the porch.

"Well, that's a lot of dust you two kicked up. If you were racing, I believe it was a tie. Let me help you down, Angel." Langley dutifully went to her side.

"I didn't think you would be coming over today. Didn't Momma tell you I was helping out at the school?" Angel asked.

"Yes, she did; but it was late when I came over, so I figured I would just wait for you. I knew you would have to come home for dinner. I hope you didn't mind that I waited." Langley walked over to Wes and extended his hand, "Wes, it's nice to see you. I haven't

116

seen you around much. I hear Margareet is keeping you busy out at her father's horse ranch."

Wes narrowed his eyes as he was tying his horse to the hitching post, "No more than your father's affairs have been keeping you busy. A man that doesn't work doesn't eat. That's what the good book says."

"I don't pay too much attention to what the good book says. My father was successful without it, and I will be too."

Angel's grip tightened on Langley's arm. "Langley, I thought you were raised Christian. Why would you say that?"

"Why would I say anything? I don't know...maybe because to me it's true."

"No Langley, it's not true. Your father might have been successful in business, but where is his soul spending eternity? Don't continue that road, Langley; or when you pass on, you'll be looking up to heaven from hell."

"Believe what you want, Angel. I personally don't see God doing anything miraculous. Look at your family's situation; God didn't and isn't helping you."

"Langley, you don't understand how God works. His time is not our time. I'm still waiting on the Lord; he knows our need before we do. His word tells me that his answer is on its way."

Langley stopped. "And what need would that be, to get out of a marriage with me? Is that your great need?" He was hurt and it showed in his eyes. Angel was sorry, but she continued to explain.

"No, Langley, to get out of a loveless marriage and to find a way for my family and the people on the ranch to be able to make a living; that's the need." Langley turned his head away from Angel and Wes.

"Well, I guess I'll just have to wait and see. I believe your momma has been keeping dinner warm for you; shall we go in?" Langley said, dismissing the subject and covering her hand with his.

Angel knew this conversation was not over; it would be brought up again. She would continue to pray for Langley, but this time it would be a prayer for his salvation. She smiled at him, "Yes, please lead us on."

117

Angel and Wes followed Langley inside to the wonderful smell of chicken pot pie. Over top of that was the sweet aroma of Momma's bread pudding. Momma and her cooking; she definitely knew the way to soften anyone's heart.

Chapter Twenty-Seven

Margareet stood staunchly before the women of the quilting group. Her eyes seemed to be fixed on Angel. Her usual soft manner and soft blue eyes now shot out sparks of contempt. Jeanette bumped Angel's arm and whispered, "What did you ever do to ruffle her feathers?"

"I'm sure I don't know. I thought we were friends."

"Well, don't look now, but here comes your friend." Jeanette bent her head and busied herself with her quilt blocks.

"Angel, I heard you were back in town. Did you have a nice time while you were in Boston? Did you meet many available young men? Well, you know... the men are all taken here: Casey and Rachael and, of course, Wes and me," Margareet said in a matter-of-fact way. That was Angel's first clue that Margareet must be worried about Wes.

"Yes, I met many young available men, all of them college educated. I've never let it concern me much if a man were available or not. When it comes right down to it, nothing is written in stone, is it, Margareet?"

Angel finished to the gasps of the ladies that were in hearing distance. "Next time you're with your man, walk a little closer to him." Angel had always regarded Margareet as a brat, a spoiled and selfish girl, and now here she stood proving it.

"Well, I never!" and with that, Margareet gathered up her dress and stomped off.

"Angel, one of these days your mouth is going to get you in trouble," Cat said, wagging her head while Jeanette just giggled. Still Cat was proud that her children stood up for themselves. The world could wipe their feet on one who didn't. She had taught her children that one could be kind and still be strong.

Mrs. Trumble banged on the podium and declared, "Ladies, we need to get started on our quilts. We will have many a cold child in need of warmth when winter sets in. Let me introduce Tana. She is from the tribe of the Plains Indians. She is going to teach us about the

119

Morning Star Quilt." Mrs. Trumble sat down and let Tana take control of the now subdued and willing women to better learn their craft.

The women gathered around Tana, welcoming her into their tiny cluster. Tana was beautiful. Her bronze skin shone and lit up her black hair and eyes. Her hair was shorn short and that surprised Angel. Yet Angel was sure she had never seen anyone so beautiful with her cut and chiseled features so strong and yet feminine. She was amazed that Tana talked English as well as her own native tongue. She admired her virtuosity.

Angel thought back to her more than eager students she had tried to teach English to when she was in Boston. Of course, with the help of Patrick and his Irish family, they had been more than successful.

There were so many Irish immigrants that couldn't read or write, and one needed the ability to read just to make it in life and not have to become indentured servants. She thought for a moment, *What was that that Patrick used to say? Oh yes, need teaches a plan.* Tana was of a different culture, but a need was a need, no matter what color it came in. She decided that after the quilting bee was over, she would ask Tana if they had such a need in her village and maybe together they could figure out a way to help them.

All of the women quieted down now and were eager to learn, a little competitive too; they all sat back and listened. Tana started out by showing them the pattern of the Morning Star quilt. Then she placed the pattern pieces on the material and finally cut out the pattern. While she worked, she told them the story of how the quilt came to be and how it was passed down to each generation to come; and it would become a part of their legacy.

"Why do you call it the morning star quilt?" inquired one of the ladies.

"In my village the camp crier would ride through the camp to awaken our people to the new day. He would call out, 'Arise! Arise! Come see the morning star!' The sight of the morning star means a new beginning, a new day. Before quilts, we had it on our clothing, our tepees and our shields." Tana stopped and rethreaded her needle.

"That's interesting, Tana. Please tell us more," Cat implored.

120

"We give them in sympathy, in times of death and at births. The quilts are given with respect and honor to those we love. In our religion it is believed that God made the stars to watch over us. We call it 'God's Eye.' It is the difference between darkness and light. If a woman sees the star in the morning, it is said that the creator has given her another day to live. What you call the Milky Way, my people call the pathway of Departed Souls. Our dead go to the Southern Star. The Great Spirit gave them power to watch over the mortals here on earth and impart spiritual blessings. So when we give a star quilt, it is with blessings and honor," Tana finished explaining as best as she could.

When Tana had given a nod to Mrs. Trumble to let her know she was done, Mrs. Trumble motioned her to a seat at the front table so she could join in on the refreshments the women had donated for the meeting. While Tana took her seat, Mrs. Trumble addressed the group,

"Thank you, Tana. I feel very enlightened, and I'm glad you took the time to explain some of your beliefs to us. I'll remember that to give a morning star quilt to someone means you're giving them a blessing. You've made it special for me. The women are grateful for you taking the time to teach them."

Tana smiled and then all the women passed the homemade goodies around and were engrossed in chatter while they relished the food. It was time for cleanup and putting away the materials, so Angel took the opportunity to talk to Tana.

"Tana, I enjoyed the telling of the morning star quilt. You speak English very well. Do all of your people have the same grasp of the English language? I taught an English language class to Irish immigrants while I was in Boston," Angel explained.

"Oh, I see. You are a teacher?" Tana asked.

"Yes, I am. That's what I went to college for. I finished with a degree in teaching."

"I learn the English language to help my people understand the English ways. They do not speak it or write it. I can ask if any would like to and then let you know."

"You can do that, but you're just a woman." Angel was

121

mystified, "Don't you have to be given permission from the males or your chief first?" Angel inquired, not knowing the Crows' customs or ways.

Tana smiled a knowing smile, then proceeded, "In my tribe, descendants for our most important roles goes to the women's lineage. Our chief is a woman."

"Oh, I'm so sorry. I didn't know your customs. That's certainly different than our customs. Here you have to talk to the man in power. Women have no legal rights, and they don't own any property. As a matter of fact, we are property. It was a miracle in itself that I even received an education."

"You are a strong and deliberate woman. In my tribe you would be considered great."

Angel was humbled. She had never thought of herself as strong; but, if she were, she got it from her mother.

"I'm so honored that you think so highly of me. I see you too as a strong woman, and I'm honored to know you. Getting back to teaching our English language to your people and chief; if they are interested, we could have class at the schoolhouse when it is finished being built. Maybe you could come with them for a while until they are comfortable."

"I would like that, and I think my people would be grateful to you, Heavenly Being."

"Oh, you mean Angel. My name is Angel; I was my mother's only girl."

"Yes, but to me and my people you will always be Heavenly Being. I will attend the classes with them, and it will be an honor. I will let you know how many will come by the next full moon." Tana smiled.

"Good, the schoolhouse should be finished by then. I look forward to it. It's been a pleasure meeting you, Tana; and your work is as beautiful as you are, my friend." Angel reached out and squeezed Tana's hand in a friendly handshake, and then they sat together and enjoyed the bounty the women had prepared.

Chapter Twenty-Eight

"Do you have everything you need, Hank? Did you get the lunches I made for you and the boys?" Momma was scurrying around and fretting over her men.

"Yes, dear. There is no need to be concerned; we have done this before," Papa said as he packed the lunches in his saddle bag. "We'll be back before you know it, I promise." Hank kissed Cat and traced her face with his fingers. He knew God would watch over the rest of his family while he was on his trip. He knew from scripture that God's eyes go to and fro; and that if God could keep watch of the entire world, it would be nothing out of his way to include watching over his family.

Papa, Toby and Tim were packed and ready. They smiled and waved until they disappeared in the dust. Cat whispered a quick prayer, the same one she'd been praying since Hank had made the decision about Angel.

"Please, God, would you help him find the answer to our problem? Don't let Angel be a part of a loveless marriage. Nothing is too big or too small for you. In your word, you ask us to cast our every care upon the Lord. That's what I've been doing; and now I'm waiting on you, Heavenly Father, and please keep my family safe. Amen."

Casey slowly rode up to the porch. "Hey, Mrs. Winters," Casey called as he dismounted his horse, "Is Angel around? If she is, I'd like to talk to her for a moment."

"Yes, Casey, she's in cleaning up the breakfast dishes. Go on in. I'm right behind you after I check on Carson and Andrew. I have to make sure they don't have any distractions and accomplish a little bit of work before Wes and Billy get here."

"Wes and Billy are going to help you out while Hank is gone? I thought Wes was pretty busy breaking horses; I wouldn't think he would be able to get away."

"Yes, apparently Wes made arrangements after Hank ran into them and asked if they could lend a hand while he was gone. They

123

Edith Gleason

stopped by last night and confirmed it. That made it easier on Hank to take the two oldest boys. I'm afraid Jeanette and Adrian are going to miss Toby, though. He always romps with the baby in the morning, and I think Jeanette sings Toby to sleep."

"You mean the baby, don't you?" Casey asked, confused.

"Oh no, I mean Toby. I think she means to sing Adrian to sleep, but Toby is the one that is the first to go to sleep. He always did like music." Cat laughed at her musings.

Casey laughed too. "I don't think Toby would appreciate us talking about it."

"Me neither, but what he doesn't know won't hurt him," Cat winked.

"What puts Angel to sleep?" Casey wondered aloud.

"I believe it's the sound of angels' wings." Cat was serious; she continued, "I believe that girl prays more than anyone I know."

"I'd say that that's a good thing. I'll see you later, Mrs. Winters." Casey tipped his hat, then went inside, and Cat went to check on her boys.

"Hey, Angel, do you have a few minutes before you rush off to do things?" Casey asked and caused Angel to jump. She was putting away dishes. "I'm sorry; I didn't mean to scare you."

"Oh you just startled me, that's all. I guess my mind was in a different place. I have time right now. Come and sit in the parlor with me. No one's in there," Angel turned and took Casey by his hand and led him in to sit down. "So what's on your mind?" she asked.

"A lot really. I've noticed that Wes is hanging around you quite a bit lately. Do you still have feelings for him?"

"You know, if that came from anyone other than you, I'd be upset and take it as prying; but since it comes from you, I know it's concern. No, I don't romanticize about him anymore, if that's what you're asking. He's a good-looking man, but that's the only way I see him. I'm just nice to him, that's all. Is there anything else on your mind?"

"Actually, I was going to ask if you'd like to see my house. I could use your input on a few things."

124

After the Rains

"When did you get a house? Did the church supply one? Has Rachael seen it? Where is Rachael? I haven't seen her since I've been home. I heard you and her were going to tie the knot."

"Whoa, Angel, I can only answer one question at a time. No, the church isn't done being built yet. They didn't supply me with a house, and I didn't ask for one. I decided I would build my own; and I've been working on it for the past three years, about as long as you were in Boston. I need to put some finishing touches here and there, and then I need to furnish it. That's where you come in. Maybe you could help me figure out what kind of furnishings I'll need. Yes, Rachael has seen it. She saw it just before she left for California a couple of months past. I've been meaning to talk to you about her."

"You don't owe me any explanation; we're just friends."

"I know I don't owe you any; I just feel I should talk to you about it. Yes, I was interested in Rachael. I was willing to marry her. I think she figured out somewhere along the way much sooner than I did that she wasn't the love of my life. I know it hurt her, but she deserved more from a marriage than that. So we both agreed to part ways. I know it hurt her when I told her I didn't think we were meant for each other, but I had to tell her; she deserved more than being second choice. No one should be second in life to anyone or anything. That's why I'm adamant that your papa will change his mind." Casey looked sternly into Angel's eyes.

"You're too kind, Casey. Any other man would've taken what she offered, but you …you never cease to surprise me, Casey. You walked away from a sure thing because you didn't love her. Langley says that marriage is just a business arrangement and that love has nothing to do with it. I'm glad that you feel love has to be on both sides. I know you must be hurting too. So do you hear from her at all?"

"Yes, she's written and she says she's happy; that's all I can ask for, and that's all there is really to say about it. That relationship is over and in the past. I've recovered and so will she. Now changing the subject, about my house, do you think you could take the time to come look at it?"

"How did you find the time to build it?"

125

"I'm not sure about that myself. I've always had a little time here and there, but then little becomes much when God is in it. So how about it; did you want to go with me?"

"When are you thinking of going?"

"Tomorrow morning, around eight, if that's okay."

"Yes that'll be fine, Casey. I can always make time for you. You just show up and I'll be ready."

"Great, I can't wait to show you the house. I'll see you later," he said somewhat excitedly. Angel was amazed by Casey. Every time she looked at him, she saw something new. Having him as a friend was a blessing for her.

Chapter Twenty-Nine

Just after daybreak, Hank, Toby and Tim arrived in Virginia City; it was a busy bustling city. Here was a place to wheel and deal, a place to be rich or a place to be broken. It was known to be a gold mining town, but all other business transactions, aboveboard or not, took place there too.

Hank had been able to secure a bit of money to buy a few more head of cattle to replace the ones he had lost during the storms, and this was the place where he could get the most for his money. He looked around and spotted a hotel.

"Toby, why don't you go over and pay for a couple days lodging? Tim will stay with me and accompany me to take a look at the livestock they have here for sale. I want to see what kind of cattle are up for sale and what kind of shape they're in."

"Yes, Papa. When I'm done, I'll meet you at the livery stable." Toby walked across the street to the hotel called the Dusty Inn.

Hank and Tim busied themselves looking over the livestock. They found that the stock for sale mainly consisted of Hereford cattle. Hank had been a breeder for years, and he knew what to look for. Broad between the eyes, the back should be full and well-rounded; and the neck should form a straight line from the head to the shoulder. Those were just a few things he looked for when he was buying cattle. Hank and Tim both agreed that most of the cattle met the requirements of good stock.

Upon further inspection, he noted that there were more than a couple of bulls which had reached the magic weight of 1800 lbs. That meant they could breed. There were also some cows that had reached their weight for breeding. Hank and Tim were in discussion over the cattle when Hank noticed that there was a group of Canadians who were also in attendance at the sale. It was the same group of men that had been there when he purchased the bison. He wondered if they were still looking for bison. Hank excused himself from Tim, who was engrossed with a passel of hogs.

"Howdy, gentlemen, it looks like a pretty big sale. From what

127

Edith Gleason

I've seen, it contains a lot of good stock. Did you find what you were looking for?" Hank asked as he approached the men.

One of the men, Jason, the most talkative of the group, spoke for them, "Not yet, but it's still early. They tell us there are more cattle coming in."

"What kind of cattle are you looking for?" Hank asked.

"Well, the last time we were here, we bought a few head of bison. We were hoping there would be some more here at this sale."

"How did you fare up in Canada?"

"They required more grazing land, of which there is plenty; and their coats got them through our cold winter. They have more beef on their limbs, so that makes up for the land they require. I remember seeing you buy some last time you were here." Jason recognized Hank as the rancher who had bought most of the bison at the last livestock auction.

"Yes I did buy quite a bit of them, thirty head, to be exact. They made it through the winter, but our spring rains washed away a lot of our grazing land. So now they're having a hard time finding food."

A thought occurred to Hank. Maybe he could offer the bison that he had purchased to these men. That would help solve the problem of not having enough land to feed his cattle. It would also give him enough money to take care of any debt that had risen up after the rains and still be able to replace some of his Hereford cattle that he had lost. He stopped for a moment and bowed his head. It was the most earnest prayer he had said in a while.

"Heavenly father, you know what we're going through here. I've tried everything, and on my own I'm failing. I even offered my daughter to an ungodly man. Forgive me, Lord; help me to right this wrong. I know you orchestrated this moment, for your word tells me you go before us. Please impress upon these Canadian ranchers' hearts to buy the bison I have in my possession. Amen."

Hank lifted his head to a group of smiling Canadian ranchers. Jason spoke, "Hank, is it? We were discussing amongst ourselves, and we were thinking since your bison aren't faring too well in Montana that you might consider selling them to us. We would be glad to pay the going rate, and that could also help you out with the

128

lack of land you are experiencing."

Hank wanted to cry for joy. This man didn't know how God had constructed this moment of time and placed the very thought in their heads to help out a doubting child, himself.

Hank couldn't help but grin; his joy was bubbling over the very top of his soul.

"I would consider it. If what you're offering is the going rate, then I believe we have a deal."

"That is the offer, Hank," Jason stated.

"Good, then I'll have my son Toby draw up the papers of sale. We can work out the details in the hotel's diner. Lunch will be on me," Hank offered his hand in a businessman's shake.

"It's a deal then." All of the men took turns shaking his hand, sealing their agreement before putting their signatures on paper. Hank told them where they were staying, and then he tipped his hat and excused himself to walk back to where he had left Tim. Toby was already there. Hank looked up toward the heavens and said, pleasingly amazed. "I knew you would provide a lamb." Looking at his sons and seeing their perplexed looks, he began to explain to his now most elated sons what had just taken place between the Canadians and himself. They all hugged and together they thanked God. They were reminded once more that God's hand had never left their lives; he had always been guiding them, through and even after the rains.

Chapter Thirty

Angel stepped into the most beautiful entranceway she had ever seen. A crystal chandelier hung above the doorway. It clinked and shimmered in the morning sunlight. The reflections of light that it cast lit the way for you to step down off the foyer and onto a polished cherry wood floor that mirrored her reflection.

Taking in the view with awe, Angel stepped down into a room which was fully opened all the way up to the cathedral ceiling. There was a stairway against the middle wall that led to the upstairs. There the rooms were next to each other, and they encircled the large open landing. In the middle of the main room was a large fireplace. Huge bay windows sat on each end of the house, which allowed you to look out and view almost every inch of the wooded green property.

Off to the left of the doorway was a long hallway, next to an open kitchen counter. On the other side of the counter was the kitchen, fully loaded with a cookstove, ice box and smaller appliances. Angel lost her breath for a moment when she saw that in the center of the kitchen stood a butcher block with shelving underneath. Casey watched as Angel's eyes widened, and her jaw dropped slightly. He took her hand and led her down the hall to the library and office.

"I'll need a place where I can pen my sermons. I thought this area would be the quietest, especially when the children arrive," Casey said as he pointed out the particulars of each room.

Angel looked up at him with her brows raised, "Children?"

Casey considered her question, "Yes, God willing, someday there will be children. I will eventually marry, Angel."

"Oh, I thought maybe you had someone's children already in mind."

Casey took Angel's hand once more and looked deep into her eyes. "I do have someone's children in mind. I know this might sound out of the blue, and I don't mean to pressure you; but I was hoping that someday the children would belong to you and me."

Angel became still. She didn't know what to say. "Casey, you

know that I'm engaged to Langley. So far nothing has happened to change that." She covered his hand with both of hers. "Oh, Casey, how can this be? We've lived next door to each other all of our lives. We laughed, played and cried together, but when did these feelings happen?"

"That's easy for me; it was the day of your birthday. When we were at the races, I saw you sitting under the tree waiting to talk to Wes. It was then that I knew if I ever saw you waiting for someone, I wanted it always to be me." Casey's voice had become soft, "I know from experience that I want no other woman in my life, except you. I'm prepared to wait for you as long as it takes."

Angel had searched her heart many times and had found strong feelings for Casey stirring within her. She had never been able to put a name on it until now; it was love. She didn't know what to do about it then, and she didn't know what to do about it now.

"Casey, when I was away in Boston, you were always in my thoughts, even when I was with Patrick. He ended up being a friend, but still it seemed I was always comparing everyone to you. Sadly, I think he knew that too and gathered that you were the reason I couldn't go with him. I didn't know it then, but I know it now; you were the reason. It was your face, no one else's, I saw before I went to sleep at night. I found myself looking for you everywhere I went." Angel looked dumbfounded as if the thought just occurred to her. "What are we going to do about this? It's so funny, when you think about it; of all the things we've shared, we never had an opportunity to share a kiss."

Casey pulled Angel close, "We can fix that part now." He lowered his face to hers and softly brushed his lips to hers. He stopped and looked into her eyes, then continued to kiss her softly over and over until Angel breathlessly placed her hand on his chest.

"We have to stop this, Casey, until there is a remedy to the problem with Langley."

"I know," Casey answered eagerly. "I just want you to know that I love you; I've always loved you, and I will always love you." Casey leaned down and gave her another kiss. "We'll continue to pray about things. I know God will take care of it. Maybe now is not

131

the time to discuss this, but I had to let you know how I felt. I just couldn't keep seeing you and not tell you."

Casey thought about the amount of time they had been gone, "I think I should get you back home before Langley sends a posse, and they all start looking for you." He took her hand and started leading her to the door.

Angel pulled Casey to a stop. "Casey, I love you too. God knew what he was doing when your father moved in next door. I don't know anything about his timing, but I do know that he is in control."

Casey smiled, pulling Angel close, then drew her into his arms and whispered above her hair, "By the way, what kind of furniture do you think will look best in here?" They both realized they hadn't accomplished what they had set out to do and laughed in spite of themselves. The couple knew those questions would wait for an answer on another day. The ride home was sobering. Casey and Angel held hands tightly, and both prayed silently as they searched their hearts for an answer.

Langley sat on the Winters' front porch. It seems he spent a lot of time there lately, always waiting for Angel. He decided that when they were married, he would make it her habit to tell him of any plans she might have. The wheels to a wagon rattled as it approached the porch. He viewed the passengers. "Another male passenger? Who is it this time?" Langley disgustingly asked himself.

Casey jumped down and gently gave Angel a lift down. They were greeted by a scowling Langley, standing rigid with his arms folded across his chest, unrelenting on the porch.

"I've been waiting for two hours for you. I can see that you have been with Casey, but just where has that been?" Langley demanded.

Casey spoke first, "She accompanied me to take a look at my house. She agreed to give me a few suggestions as to the furnishings."

"I would think my fiancée could speak for herself," Langley said, ignoring Casey and looking directly at Angel. He was angry with her. He knew she didn't know of his coming today, but it seemed she could have given him a second thought in considering he might drop by and who she spent her time with. After all, she was *his* fiancée.

"I'm sorry, Langley; I didn't know you were going to visit today. I would have made provisions to stay home. I didn't mean to inconvenience you. Please come in and we'll discuss your reason for visiting today."

"I'm going to head out to the site of the school building. I promised I'd be there to help them raise it. I'll see you later, Angel. You have a good day, Langley." Casey climbed up in his wagon and waved goodbye.

Langley followed Angel inside. When they were seated, he began, "Just why is it that you're spending so much time with Casey? And what did he mean by, 'See you later'? Doesn't he know you're engaged?" Angel sighed; she was so discouraged by this relationship that she didn't know what to say anymore. She prayed as she looked into Langley's eyes. It was then she saw hurt.

"I'm sorry if I hurt you, Langley. That was never my intention. I'm going to be honest with you. I do have feelings for Casey that are stronger than friendship. I wish I could say I was sorry, but how does one apologize for feeling love for another?"

Langley was quiet. "You don't apologize for love. Just tell me why it isn't me whom you love?"

"I don't know much about these things myself. I just know I didn't choose to have these feelings, yet they still exist. I think God has a lot to do with who we fall in love with; as a matter of fact, I know he does. There's nothing wrong with you, Langley. I just know in my heart that you're not the one I'm supposed to marry. I care for you; I will always care for you, but it will be as a friend, nothing more."

"I certainly appreciate your candor. Honesty is a must in a relationship. So you're going to continue this friendship with Casey even after we are married and without my approval."

"No, Langley. He and I both understand God's views on marriage, and we will only be seeing one another as friends."

Langley seemed at ease with her answer, only because he knew her faith in God kept her from letting him down; and Langley depended on it. *It was funny,* he thought to himself, *in a way I am depending on God too.*

133

"I just wanted to let you know that I will be out of town for the rest of the week on business and for you to not expect me on the usual days."

"Thank you for letting me know. Papa should be back by then," Angel informed Langley.

"Yes, when he gets back, we'll have some things to discuss." Langley excused himself on that; and, carrying a heavy heart, Angel escorted him to the door.

After bidding him a good day, Angel closed the door softly. She stood there resisting the strongest urge she had ever had, to just pick up her feet and run so far away and so fast that no one would ever find her; but she knew that would only hurt the people she loved. Why was it that she couldn't be cold-hearted and uncaring, like so many others she knew, and not care about anyone but herself? A small voice spoke to her heart, "I went to the cross. I could've called thousands of Angels, but I died alone; and I did it for all of my children."

Angel regretted her thoughts; and with tears in her eyes, she bowed her head and asked for forgiveness from Jesus. Yes, she felt as if she were suffering; but she knew that with Jesus, the suffering would end and through all of it, she would never be alone.

Chapter Thirty-One

The schoolhouse stood tall and sturdy with its new red paint shining brightly in the midday sun. The school actually had a bell tower, equipped with a bell donated from Virginia City. The school house was beautiful with its new wooden floors and shiny windows.

The construction team had designed it with three rooms: a coat room and two large class rooms. It was her request, so Angel could separate the older children from the younger ones. Looking over the size of the rooms, a thought occurred to her: with all these children, she would need an assistant.

Everyone had left for the day, leaving Angel with straightening up and completing the finishing touches. Unaware of what was going on around her, Angel stood on a stepstool, measuring the windows for curtains, which she would make with the material she had brought from Boston. She was startled when she heard scrapings of boots on the floor, along with a male voice speaking out from behind her.

"What, are you all alone in this great big schoolhouse?" Wes asked as he came toward her, looking over the room. "The school looks great, Angel. They did a good job."

"If I remember right, you helped too. Yes, it does look great. I was thinking that with as many children as I am expecting to attend, I'll probably have to hire on an assistant to help me." Angel continued writing down the measurements she had just taken.

"When is opening day for the children?"

"I'd say next Monday. By then I should have all the finishing touches done and their assignments in order."

"How many students do you think you'll have?"

"I figured possibly about fifty."

"Yep, you'll definitely need some help. If you don't mind me asking, when the schoolhouse is finished being built, is Langley going to let you teach?"

"He says that no wife of his is going to work, but I'm not his wife, for right now, that is."

"No, you're not. You know, Angel, I'll be coming into money after I seal the deal and marry Margareet. Maybe I'll have enough where I could take care of your family's financial woes and you. Surely I must be more desirable to be with than Langley," Wes said, slowly stroking his hand up and down Angel's arm.

Feeling as if a snake just crawled down her back, Angel felt a shiver go up her spine and stepped immediately away from his touch. "Whether you are or aren't desirable doesn't have any bearing on whom I'll be married to. For some reason you're under the assumption that I am up for barter. I'll have you know that I'm not." Angel's eyes began to tear and she began to shake.

"Who said anything about you being my wife? I won't need two." Wes grabbed at her but became distracted and missed when he heard another male voice speak up behind him.

"Wes, I thought you were a better man than that," Hank stood behind Wes with a scowl on his face and his hands curled up in fists. "Tell me I didn't just hear you making an unkind offer to my daughter, and I'll let you walk out of here with all of your teeth and your face still intact."

Wes jerked his body around to face Hank. "I'm sure you misunderstood me. I was just discussing with her her unfortunate circumstance and offering her another way out."

"Candy-coat it any way you want, it was still degrading to my daughter's integrity, not to mention her faith. I'll kindly ask you to leave, since it's apparent you don't seem to have any understanding of what is right and what is wrong."

"Oh, I understand perfectly. It's all gravy when you come up with a deal for your daughter, but not for others to do the same. That's a double standard, isn't it, even for a Christian?" Wes was smirking now; he knew his words stung Hank.

"A man wouldn't be under God's grace or mercy if he never learned some of the things he chose to do were wrong. I believe God still sees me as teachable. Not that it is any of your business, but what I tried to do with Angel's life was wrong. God taught me that and I came to apologize to her." Hank was looking past Wes now and into his baby daughter's eyes that were wet with shedding tears. "Do

136

you forgive me, Angel?" he asked, stepping closer and holding his arms out to her.

"Oh Papa, how could I not? But what about Langley and how will our family make it financially?" Angel asked, wrapping her arms around Hank.

"God provided a lamb. I'm so sorry I ever put you through this, baby. I guess I was the rich man that couldn't leave my possessions and follow Christ. God knew that and showed me my wicked ways. Even now I still repent." Hank dropped his head into his daughter's hair. His body shook with sobs as he cried out to his God and to his daughter for forgiveness.

Angel and Hank stood with their arms wrapped around each other and prayed together for a long time. They had a lot to talk to the father about and each other. While they stood in prayer, they didn't take notice of Wes, who took it as an opportunity to quickly make his exit. He would have to do some fast talking when he got home and faced Margareet and her father.

After prayer, Hank wiped his eyes. "I should get going; I have some matters to discuss with Langley and my wife to ask forgiveness from too. How about you, Angel? Are you done here?" Hank asked, after looking around and seeing that Wes had made a quick exit.

Angel was wiping her eyes and laughing in relief. "Yes, I'm done for now. I think Momma will be pleased to hear what you have to say, and I'm pretty sure she's going to say it was a long time coming." Angel was quiet for a moment, and then she asked, "Papa?"

"Yes, Angel," Hank said as he was putting back on his hat.

"Thank you for interrupting Wes. I thought he was a good person; I guess I was wrong. Shouldn't we let Margareet and her father know about Wes's behavior?"

"I think they'll find out soon enough on their own. He's chosen the wrong path. It appears he had us both hornswoggled. That was our first mistake, Angel. In God's word, he says there is none that is good, no not one. Wes proved that today and probably other countless times that only God saw. The best thing for us to do is just put it behind us. People like that tell on themselves without any help from us. Let's go, baby girl; it's getting late." Hank picked up

Edith Gleason

Angel's belongings, and they headed home to make things right. Hank was preparing his heart to ask forgiveness from those he had hurt, and Momma and Toby were among them.

Chapter Thirty-Two

"Hank, Hank!" Cat squealed as she threw up her hands and ran towards her husband and sons. No sooner had their feet reached the kitchen than Cat had her arms wrapped around them. "I missed all of you, so much."

Her men hugged her back and kissed her cheeks. Jeanette ran to greet Toby with Adrian swinging on her hip. Just as she reached him, Adrian leaped from her to his papa. Catching him in midair, Toby swung him up and down to his glees of delight. Finally, resting him on his arm, he grabbed Jeanette and gave her a deep, solid kiss.

"I missed you, Jeanette, and Adrian." He looked at his boy, "I missed your mama singing you lullabies. I bought both of you a trinket from Virginia City; it's in my satchel."

Jeanette squeezed her husband's arm gently, "The gifts can wait until later; let's go inside. I think you guys could use a little rest and sit-down for a bit. It's been a long ride; and I'm sure you've all got some catching up to do and some stories to tell."

"I'll unpack the horses and put them in the barn. You and Papa go ahead and tend to the women folk. I know how they all have their needs," Tim teased his family.

"You, Tim, just come here; I've got a kiss for you also, albeit brotherly, but we missed you too," Jeanette giggled, and then she pecked Tim on his cheek.

"Hey, hey, that's enough; you need to get your own little brother." Toby pulled Jeanette away from his little brother and toward the house, then called to Tim and told him thanks for taking care of the horses.

Hank held back and ushered the rest on, saying he had things to discuss with Cat. They sat down in the swing on the front porch; and when they were alone, Hank began, "Cat, I've sinned. The Bible says, 'When a man hurts the heart of a woman, God doesn't hear his prayers.' Forgive me, Cat, for not listening to you about how God would answer our dilemma. I always believed God would send a lamb. I got ahead of God and tried to make Angel the lamb. I was

139

wrong, but God did send a lamb; he gave us the bison for just this time of need."

He paused, then continued, "You see, Cat, the bison need more land to graze, even though they produce more beef. Due to the rains, we lost a lot of our grazing land, but we still had cattle and bison. At the livestock sale, the Canadians were there except there weren't any bison for sale. That's what they were looking for. I asked the Lord and felt led to offer them mine. That's what the Lord wanted. The Canadians gave me the going rate per head. Cat, God sent a lamb after all." Caitlyn was in tears, not from sadness, but from joy.

"Oh, Hank, I prayed so hard for you. I trusted you would listen to the heavenly father; it just took the right circumstance." She was holding Hank's hand and he squeezed hers tighter. "We have to tell Angel; won't she be happy!"

"I did tell her, Cat, and I asked her for forgiveness too. You know, Cat; we raised some pretty remarkable children."

Cat placed her head on Hank's shoulder.

"Yes, Hank, with the Lord's help, we did."

"While we were in Virginia City, Toby came up with some ideas on what to do with our now barren grazing land. We can cultivate it and grow different crops. The soil is rich and should produce plenty of grains. With the railroad in full force, we'll have a way to transport the grain. I hear they'll be building a grinding mill in town, so that will help too. God sure is good. He just keeps on taking care of us; even when we don't see what's coming, he does." Hank was excited.

"I should never have wavered in my faith. The good book says that, 'Behold, the eye of the Lord is upon them that fear him, upon them that hope in his mercy.' And I am definitely hoping in his mercy." Hank then went over the plans he and Toby had discussed. "I'll go over and talk to Langley tomorrow. We need to pray about that. I don't like to see anyone hurt; and I think he may have some sort of feelings for Angel, even though he would never admit to it."

The couple stayed on the porch, swinging as they watched the burning embers of a summer day draw to an end. Hank thought that he had never seen a prettier sunset. Serenely the couple smiled as they listened to the children's banter and laughter coming from inside their home. It was good to be home and content in where the Lord leads you.

Cat reached over and patted Hank's hand, then whispered, "In whichever state I am in, I have learned therewith, to be content."

*****

"I was expecting you, Hank. Please sit down," Langley offered the leather chair across from his desk. "Our deal is approaching an end. So what do you propose our next step should be?"

"I'm assuming we're discussing Angel." Hank looked him in the eyes, "Do you even love her, Langley?" Hank wanted and waited for his answer.

"Hank, we're both businessmen. When has love ever had anything to do with a business deal?" Langley seemed confused.

"So you still want my Angel as part of the deal; you want her as payment?"

"I thought we had an agreement and that you understood? I care for Angel, if that makes you feel better; and I'm sure love will come later. She's a woman, Hank; and in this day and age, she goes where we put her, whether it is as a wife or as a payment," Langley stated distantly, gathering his legal papers for Hank to sign.

"I put her in God's hands when she was born, and God has other plans for her. I've come to find it doesn't include you or me. I'm sorry, Langley; we no longer have a deal. I made Angel my family's sacrifice, but Jesus already paid that price. I was the rich man for a while. I was holding onto earthly goods instead of leaving it all behind and following the Lord. I forgot that the father owns it all, and it's just on loan to us. Angel belongs to the Lord. Only he is in control. God allows things and sometimes orchestrates them, but in everything, once again, all I can know is that God is in control; he's sovereign."

Langley was at a loss for words. "If God truly loves you, why did he let you suffer? Why does he let anyone suffer?"

"Well, Langley, there is sin in the world. God can't look at sin, God is not mocked, and no sin goes unpunished. Did I sin? Yes. We all sin. The Bible says there is none that is good, no, not one. Where there is sin, there is punishment. God is still in control. He can

141

deliver us or walk through it with us; either way he's there. In his
word he says, 'if you love your children, you will chastise them.' We
are his children and he chastises. He took me away from my family
and all the fretting I was doing; it was then I became still. That's
when God took care of it, and I heard his words. I feel I need to
explain that God gave my family a different way to do our business.
He helped us to see we could use what we had available, and he took
Angel out of the equation."

"Are you sure you're not making a mistake? I won't make this
offer again." Langley looked sternly and unbelievingly at Mr.
Winters.

"I am sure. I'm sorry if you have any hurt feelings; for that I ask
your forgiveness, but our business dealing is over." Hank stood and
gathered his hat in his hands.

"You Christians and your God; are you people delusional? The
only answers in this world are the things you can hold in your hands,
and it looks to me as if your hands are empty."

"That's where faith would come in. God's arms are wide open to
you and anyone; Langley, talk to him." Hanks words were soft as
they fell on Langley's ears.

"Anyone can look at my life and see that it is good, and I don't
pray!" Langley was defiant.

"One day you will pray. My prayer for you is that earth is not
your heaven. Langley, the Father waits for you; he sent his only son
Jesus to die for you. He suffered alone and went to the cross alone.
All you have to do is whisper his name and he's there, right where
you are. Don't forget that, Langley; God is only a prayer away."
Hank stood to his feet and, placing his hat on his head, prepared to
leave.

Langley had listened intently. He had great respect for Hank. He
wondered how such a strong man could depend on something he
could not see. Maybe there was substance to this God stuff. Langley
looked Hank in the eye; he was emotional and had been moved by
Hank's words.

"One day, Hank, maybe I'll trust in him too, just like you do."
Langley's voice was choked with emotion.

"Don't make it one day too late, Langley. I'll be praying for you." Hank nodded, then turned and walked out of Langley's office. "Lord," he prayed to himself, "he's a good young man and he needs you. Don't give up on him just yet. Amen."

After Hank left, Langley's heart was heavy. By all means, he should have been angry with Hank for not going through with the deal. He'd been scorned by people before and always lashed out at them and ended with revenge. This time it was different; there was comfort in the words that Hank spoke. Langley dropped his head on his hands. He was alone. Hank didn't understand what it was like to be alone. He had all of his children and his wife; what did he know about being all alone? Even when his father was alive, he was left to himself.

Hank's words came back of how Jesus suffered and died alone, so that he would know what loneliness was to man. He made a way for us to be saved and to always be near us.

Langley looked up, "Where were you, God, all that time? Did you see me crying? Did you see me playing by myself and even talking to myself? Were you listening? Are you listening now? Then hear this now!"

Langley cried, "I don't want to be alone anymore!" Langley's head dropped again; and he cried until there were no tears left, and his eyes were swollen shut. He begged the heavenly father for forgiveness in the things that he had done and then asked for peace so that he could sleep at night. The one thing he wanted most he didn't have to ask for again, for somewhere inside, Langley found the assurance he would never be alone again. He knew that Jesus was the friend that would be there, no matter what he faced in this life.

God's peace was overwhelming, and Langley found new tears of joy that dripped onto the pages of a business deal, causing the ink to run the words together, a deal God had made no longer valid when he placed it under the blood. Langley smiled. He finally had peace. He found it in the scriptures where Jesus promised, "I will never leave you nor forsake you." In Langley's heart, his new faith led him to believe those words.

Chapter Thirty-Three

"After all this rebuilding, it's time to have a little fun. It was nice of Langley to offer his barn for tonight's happenings. He sure is a changed man," Toby noted to his family, as they headed out the door for the dance. "You sure look pretty, Jeanette," he said, pulling her close and kissing her. "You too, little man. Come here and Daddy will carry you. You want to ride up front with Grandpa and Nana?" Toby asked as he hoisted Adrian up to Hank.

"Yeah, that's a big boy. He can help Grandpa drive the team." Hank placed his grandson on the seat between him and Caitlyn. "There," he said, placing Adrian's hands on the reins. "Now you're the driver."

"The rumor has it that Toby and Jeanette will be blessed with another child soon," Caitlyn said as if musing, but loud enough so all of the family in the wagon could hear. The news caused whoops and hoorays with laughter and teasing toward the expecting couple.

"Papa, did you teach Toby that?" Tim teased; he was sitting next to Toby. Toby gave him a quick nudge in the ribs and then headlocked and wrestled Tim to the floor of the wagon. Momma still fussed with her grown-up boys about them getting mussed up before they got there.

Papa took it in good humor and replied to his wrestling boys, "There are some things you just can't teach. I hear it comes natural." The family giggled and bantered with one another for the short ride to Langley's barn. Angel had let the family know that she and Casey would be coming later after they had gone over to the schoolhouse to drop some supplies off.

The townspeople were excited. With all the preparation and hard work that had gone into the barn dance, it held promise of being an interesting evening.

*****

"Are you nervous, Angel?" Casey asked as he lifted her down from the buggy.

"No, I'm just a little apprehensive. I'm sure Langley is okay by

144

now; I'm just not sure what to say to him."

"Just pray about it. God already had this meeting in mind, so relax and let God be the head of your conversations. Besides, I'll be next to you the whole time, so just lean on me." Casey took her arm and walked her to the entrance, where Langley stood greeting the guests.

Even from a distance, Langley recognized Angel's beauty. He had always appreciated that one specific detail about her. He knew that the Lord had someone special in mind for him too; he just needed to wait on him. In his heart he just hoped she'd be as pretty as Angel. "Evening, folks, you're both looking very fine. I hope you enjoy your evening. Please be my guest. The refreshments are inside; just help yourself."

Casey shook Langley's hand, "Thank you, Langley, you don't know how much this means to the people of the town and all of us. If you need help with anything, let me know."

Langley smiled, "I will let you know and you're very welcome."

Casey and Angel stepped inside the decorated barn. They found there that most of the people had a partner and were already dancing to the dance caller's directions. Casey grabbed her hand and swung her around to face him, "Shall we dance, Miss Angel?"

"We shall," Angel answered in a gasp as she was swung to the floor. Looking back at Langley, she smiled and nodded. She whispered a prayer of thanks that the Lord had spared his feelings, and that was her last thought as she was swung about the dance floor by an eager Casey who wanted to dance.

*****

Wes stood leaning against a barn pole as he watched Casey lead Angel around the floor. *So she got out of marriage with Langley, only to be hooked up to the preacher boy. Why is it that I wasn't even considered as a contender? I'm just as good, if not better than him.* Wes bitterly thought to himself. *I'm good enough to work for the Winters, but not good enough for their daughter. Well, we'll see what she really thinks of me tonight. I'll have money soon, and then I'll have my pick of any woman I want. But tonight Angel is the one I want, and I'm sure she will find me irresistible. After all, there will*

145

be at least one opportunity where Casey won't be around and that she'll be left alone.

"What are you doing over here? Father and I have been looking for you. Don't you want to dance?" Margareet asked, noticing the slight anger in Wes's face as she approached.

He stood up and forced a pleasing smile for his fiancée. "How could I not want to dance with the most beautiful flower of all flowers?"

"Oh Wes, you're such a charmer. Just being here with you makes me the envy of all the other girls."

"We'll dance the next song." Margareet was satisfied with the answer Wes gave her.

Wes noted on several occasions that it didn't take much to make her happy. All he had to do was feed her ego and not to mention her attention span was that of a bee. Wes had always thought of her as easy on the eyes; he just didn't find her very exciting. She didn't have the fire that Angel had. He'd always liked a good fight. That's why he was so good on the horse ranch; he could break and then race any horse. Margareet and her daddy's money could never change that he was a good horse trainer. As a matter of fact there were lots of things, unbeknownst to them, that they would never change about Wes.

*****

After they had danced the third song, Casey led Angel outside to cool off and be refreshed by the cool night air. "The air feels so good. I haven't danced like that in ages," Angel said, waving her small fan.

"Lord help me, even when you're too warm, you're still breathtaking. Would you like me to get you something to drink, Angel?" Casey couldn't help but see her beauty. He knew it wasn't just her outer shell but the beauty that shone from within. He knew it would take a different sort of man to not see it.

Angel smiled and blushed. "You really need to stop feeding my ego. My head is going to be so big it won't fit in any of my bonnets. I thank you, but you're really being too kind, Casey."

"I'm not trying to be kind; I'm just appreciating the beauty God placed on you. Now would you like me to go get some refreshments

146

for you? While I'm gone, it will give you a chance to give your feet a rest too."

"I was thinking that after I've cooled off, I'd like to go and talk to Tana. I'm so pleased she came. Of course, I had to promise to attend their Summer Sun Dance. I hear it's pretty festive," Angel said, her mind already busy making future plans.

"You're a busy girl; even though your feet are resting, your brain is working overtime. Well, maybe I'll escort you. All those good-looking braves fawning over you; I think you'll need some strong protection, you know, against all the wild life they might have in camp," Casey seemed to say as a comfort.

"Wild life, and are you a bear?" Angel tilted her head to the side innocently.

"Who, me? All right, you caught me. I want to come along to protect you from the braves. You can't blame a man for trying." He laughed, then said, "That was good of Tana to ask her people about tutoring them in English. She's bringing twelve that are interested?"

"Yes, and that's a good start. There are so many fences that need mending amongst our people. Maybe it will help to at least break down the communication barrier. I'm praying it does."

"I believe any little bit will help. Now I think I'll go get you that drink I promised."

"Yes please, I'd love some punch," Angel said, continuing to fan herself. After Casey promised to be right back, she found a bench and sat down. It was fall and the leaves had already turned. Angel watched as they fluttered slowly to the ground. The night air was cool on Angel's face and it felt good. She leaned her head back against the bench and closed her eyes. She hummed softly along to the music, which seem to float out of the barn.

"You're looking as pretty as always," Wes said, trying not to slur his words, as he stood in front of Angel. Angel's eyes snapped open as she looked about for other people, and realizing she was alone, she warily brought her attention back to Wes.

"Not for long; Casey said he will be right back." She felt the need to assure him. "Where is Margareet? I noticed she was looking for you earlier; did she find you?" Angel tried to distract him from

147

Edith Gleason

what his eyes were already telling her.

"She found me and now she lost me. I have something you might want. It's something that I didn't get to deliver to you at the schoolhouse the other day." Wes suddenly reached down and, grabbing Angel, pulled her to her feet. His fingers dug into the soft flesh of her arms as he jerked her roughly to his chest and, with bruising force, kissed her hard on her mouth.

With all her might, Angel pushed at Wes, while kicking at his shins. She squirmed and tried to yell for help; but he had a strong grip on her, and his mouth was still crushing hers. She felt as if her efforts all seemed for naught when a hand tapped Wes on the shoulder. Surprised and startled, it caused him to jerk about, standing with his mouth agape, staring into the angry eyes of Casey. He didn't take notice of the fist that flew into his jaw and another into his stomach that sent him splaying to the ground.

"Get up and I'll do it again," Casey promised as he stood over top of Wes. Both of his hands curled in tight fists at his sides. "That's not how you treat a lady. And it looks as if it's time someone taught you a lesson."

Wes wiped blood from the side of his mouth. Holding his hand in front of him to view the damage, he sneered, "So the preacher boy can deliver a punch. Are you the one that thinks he's going to teach me a lesson, Casey? Well, I hope you can take a punch as well as you give them." Wes scuffled to his feet. When he finally stood, he looked around to the surprised and angry faces of Margareet and her father, the townspeople, and Angel's angry family.

"I think you've worn out your welcome here. You need to dust yourself off, take what you have left of your dignity, if you even have any, and leave," Casey demanded.

Margareet's father stepped in front of Casey, "Leave town and don't come back. You've embarrassed my daughter and our family's good name for the last time. Don't bother going back to the ranch; everything you had I gave to you. I wouldn't be much of a gentleman if I didn't let you leave with at least a horse and the shirt on your back, so those you may have. My ranch hands will escort you to the end of town. Don't even think of coming back, because it will be *my*

After the Rains

justice waiting for you then; and next time I won't be as forgiving."

Margareet, who was standing behind her father, argued, "But I love him, Father."

Putting his arm gently around his only daughter, he offered, "There will be other opportunities for you to fall in love. This one's not worth your time." Somewhat satisfied, Margareet dabbed at her eyes and quieted her sniffles, while her father's ranch hands pushed a stumbling Wes toward the horses. Margareet's father gathered his little girl in his arms and pushed through the gathered crowd. With words of comfort, holding his head high, he then walked her slowly to their carriage.

The fight was over, and Wes had been dutifully escorted from town. The people disbursed and Casey went to Angel. "Are you all right? He didn't hurt you, did he?" Casey searched Angel's eyes and face, surveying for damage and waiting for an answer.

"No, he didn't hurt me, just my pride is all." Her hands were on his forearms, for Casey's hands were holding her shoulders, she realized, to keep her standing and to keep her from shaking. "Thank you, Casey. When I think about my life, I think you've been rescuing me ever since I was little. Aren't you getting tired of being my hero?"

"Never, how could anyone ever tire of you?" Casey pulled her into the circle of his arms. "Until the day you tell me to go away, I'll always be there for you." He held her and softly stroked her hair. Standing quietly in his embrace, Angel melted with relief; she felt safe there. The sound of people clearing their throats caused them to remember where they were. Casey loosened his embrace on Angel as they both turned and looked sheepishly into her family's faces.

Hank spoke softly, "I think that's enough excitement for the day and for the rest of the year. I think everyone would agree. What do you children say to helping Langley clean up the barn and going home?"

"I think that's a great idea, Papa," Angel replied, smiling at him.

"I've already thanked Langley so, after we take care of the mess inside, let's hop aboard the wagon and roll out of here." Cat and her children laughed at Papa's wording, but they were all in agreement as they called it a night at the barn dance.

149

Edith Gleason

Chapter Thirty-Four

"Why didn't you tell me Wes tried to put moves on you before? I would've been watchful of him, and I certainly wouldn't have left you alone where he could've hurt you." Casey was upset.

"Papa thought he took care of it. I wasn't trying to keep it from you; I just thought it was taken care of. I'm sorry I didn't tell you about it when it happened; but, on the other hand, you can't be everywhere I am. I have to take care of myself sometimes," Angel said, trying to make Casey feel better.

"That's alright. Wes is definitely taken care of now. It's a shame that Margareet had to be hurt like that, though."

"Margareet is beautiful. She'll bounce back and be the belle of the ball in no time. I have always envied her beauty."

"Women surprise me; no, I'll take that back. It's you that surprises me, Angel, with how you view yourself," Casey said with a laugh. "How could you envy anyone when you're beautiful yourself?"

"I guess beauty is in the eye of the beholder. I appreciate you beholding me, Casey." Angel grinned, knowing she was making light of their conversation.

"Okay, I'll change the subject. Langley took all of it well, didn't he? I'd say his behavior shows he is a changed man for sure."

"Yes, he was the perfect host. He has changed, and only God could make that difference. I'm glad for him."

"You're not questioning your answer to him, are you? It's still no, isn't it?" Casey asked, looking worried. Angel looked at Casey. He was handsome with his rugged good looks. Yet he looked like a lost boy before her.

"No, I'm not questioning my decision. I'm just thrilled that another friend found the Lord. Right now I'm happy just standing here with you." Angel gave his hand a little squeeze. "Did I tell you my cousin Lyndee wrote and said that she would be visiting here in about a week? I can't wait for you to meet her. She's a real pleasure to be around."

150

"Oh, is she my long-awaited, and much talked about, rival in mischievous games? I can't wait to meet her either. We'll have to compare our stories; that should prove to be interesting and make the coming seasons more festive."

Angel rolled her eyes and smiled, "You two will be birds of a feather."

Chapter Thirty-Five

Angel looked around the classroom. Soon it would be full and lively with the voices of forty children in attendance. She set out the books with their slate and chalk. She walked over to the large chalkboard and wrote her name in big letters across it. The student's ages would be between seven and sixteen. Angel was excited. She was glad that Lyndee had offered to help her when she arrived here in Montana because she was a bit nervous today.

She looked at her watch that Papa had given her. It was 7 a.m., so she walked over to the rope and pulled it. The school bell clanged out a glorious sound to begin the first day of school.

Angel stood on the front porch and watched as the children seemed to pour out from behind the trees. She greeted each of her students and asked them their names as each one stepped up. She knew she would enjoy getting to know all of them. Susan and Melee were the smallest; Jeff and Jed were her oldest students in attendance; but, of course, her favorite would have to be her little brother, Carson.

At the beginning of class, the students all introduced themselves and stated their favorite hobbies. The older boys all seemed to like fishing and hunting, while the older girls liked to read and embroider. Angel explained that those were actually necessities and encouraged them to write or draw to find a creative way to express themselves. The smaller children liked coloring and stories. Angel instructed them to come up with one of their own stories and include themselves as characters.

By the end of the day, she was exhausted. The older girls stayed a little after and helped her with cleanup. Angel once again stood on the front porch and waved goodbye to her students. She thanked the girls who had stayed to help out. She gathered her twenty apples that she had received from her students and smiled as she put them in a basket. She decided she would make some apple tarts as a treat for her students. She was lost in her thoughts and lessons when Casey walked in.

"I hope you're thinking about me, and that's what's making you smile," Casey said as he walked over to her and started to gather her belongings for home.

"You know it. Thinking of you always makes me smile. What are you doing here?" Angel asked, noticing the time and that she knew he had a full load of work of his own to do at the church.

"I was thinking of old times. I would like to be the one to walk the prettiest girl home from school and, if she would, for her to let me carry her books."

"Well, right now I'm the only girl here, so I guess you mean me. It would be my pleasure to be walked home by the best- looking boy in or out of school," Angel said as Casey put his arm around her and gently led her out the door.

"By the way, I will be walking you home from now on. So don't go getting any ideas about any other boys."

"I would never do that. Lead on, kind sir." Angel took his hand as he helped her down the steps and up into his carriage. "I think I could live with this arrangement, can you?"

"You needn't ask; I wouldn't have proposed it if I didn't want to do it. Now tell me about your first day of school."

Angel knew the reason Casey did things for her was because he cared about her. It was hard, but she tried not to read any other meaning into the concern he had shown her. They talked all the way home to Hank's ranch, so engrossed in their discussion that they never once paused to look at things that they passed by.

*****

Sunday morning Angel woke to Carson's squeals of excitement as he ran up and down the stairs yelling, "Lyndee's here! Lyndee's here!"

Angel quickly donned her robe and slippers and ran to greet her best cousin. Meeting on the stairwell, they grabbed each other and hugged to loud laughter and squeals. Angel finally let her go and stepped back.

"I believe there is less of you to hug," she said, looking her cousin over.

"Yes, you are correct. Yet there appears to be more of you. I

153

Edith Gleason

think you must be eating Aunt Cat's cherry pies," Lyndee laughed.

Cat spoke out, "Oh sure, blame the little woman! I can take it; I got big shoulders. Come here, you little rascal." Cat pulled Lyndee into her bear hug. That's what her children called it when they couldn't breathe.

"That's enough, Momma," Angel said, pulling at Lyndee and retrieving her from Cat's hug. "Come on upstairs; I've got so many things to ask you. Did you have a good trip? Was Tim on time to get you? He better have been; we all know how he likes to lollygag around." Angel continued to throw questions at Lyndee all the way up the stairs.

Hank watched the two girls go up, then smiled and said to Cat, "It's gonna be hard to separate those two." She nodded in agreement as she and Papa sat down for coffee.

*****

The church was full as Casey ended his sermon with rousing "Amens" from the parishioners. Angel and Lyndee had seated themselves in the front row. After the service, Lyndee looked around the congregation and spotted Langley. She grabbed Angel's arm and whispered, "Angel, there is Langley; take me over so I can talk to him."

Angel looked at her in surprise. "Since when did you become shy?"

"Come on, come on," Lyndee begged.

"Fine, follow me." Angel gave in and weaved through the crowd, with Lyndee hanging onto her arm. Finally, making their way through the crowd, they stood in front of Langley.

"Langley, you remember my cousin Lyndee from Boston; she's here to visit and help me out at the school."

Langley smiled at Lyndee, "Yes, of course I do. I never forget a pretty face. How are you? Did you have a good trip?" After answering Langley's questions, both he and Lyndee were off and running without any help from Angel, so she stepped quietly away and left them to their conversation. As soon as she stepped away, Casey was by her side.

"Do you think they would like to have dinner at my house? I already have a roast in the oven. How about you ask them when they

154

come up for air?" Casey asked.

Angel thought to herself, then asked, "How did you know I was thinking that? Are you sure you have enough for a couple more people like Langley and Lyndee?"

"There you go, questioning a man that knows his food," Casey teased. "Of course I have enough. I'll go with you and extend an invitation to them; that way it will look like both of our ideas."

"You know what? You go and I'll wait for you. That way it will look like your idea. I'm hungry, so be quick," Angel coaxed. Casey laughed and left her to wait for him at the back of the church. She watched with amusement as Casey came back with Lyndee and Langley in tow.

"Let's go; dinner waits." Casey ushered them towards his house.

Casey escorted Angel to the door. He wanted to see her reaction to his house. Opening the door, Casey stepped back to allow Angel's entrance. Angel stepped inside Casey's beautiful home and was pleased when she saw that he had taken her direction in choosing his furniture. After discussing the furniture and the layout of the house, Angel's attention turned toward the kitchen. The aromas that were wafting from the kitchen caused her belly to rumble.

"Wow, something smells delicious. I didn't know you could cook, Casey. You're just full of surprises, aren't you?"

"I go according to what my pa always said, 'Keep 'em guessing, son. That's how you keep the women on their toes and trouble at bay.' I've always taken good advice," Casey said with a wry smile; then he wrapped Angel's arm around his and escorted her to her seat.

The rest of his guests followed suit and seated themselves beside one another at the table. They enjoyed the dinner set before them, and they all conversed and laughed through the entire dinner, only stopping once in a while to catch their breath.

If anyone from town had peered in the window and seen the dinner guests and knew each other's story, might have thought these couples were in an awkward situation; but Langley was a changed man. Plus he seemed to have eyes only for Lyndee. Angel and Casey just smiled, enjoying each other's company, and sat back and let nature take its course.

155

Chapter Thirty-Six

"I am so thankful for your help, Lyndee. I don't know how I did it without you. The students are so good and patient, the girls are so helpful cleaning up, and the boys help me when they can, with the little ones, that is. Now if I could get them to stop pulling the older girls' braids," Angel said, flipping through books and writing down the week's lessons.

Lyndee sat across from her doing the same thing. "Yes, they really are good students. I've seen how anxious they are to pitch in and help. I think they appreciate the effort you put out on their behalf."

"I feel like this is what I was born to do, that teaching has always been my Godly calling. It's a blessing that the children are so eager to learn. I've also seen how they've taken a shine to you too. Have I told you how much I really appreciate all of your help? You must know that I'm going to miss you when you go. Have you decided how much longer you will be staying, Lyndee?"

"I've been thinking about that. I've grown attached to Langley, but I'm not sure how or what he thinks of me. He sure isn't the same man that came to Boston, is he?"

"No, he's not, Lyndee. God's word says, 'For ye were sometimes darkness; but now are ye light in the Lord. Walk as children of light.' I believe Langley has chosen to walk in the light. Even his business deals are upfront and honest; and, since you've arrived here, he doesn't seem to be as lonely. All I see is that you're good for him, Lyndee."

"My goodness, he's all that and handsome too," Lyndee twirled around and acted as if she were swooning, much to Angel's delight.

"Is Langley coming to get you tonight?"

"Yes, he should be here around seven. He said he has some things to discuss with me. I think he's going to ask me to stay a while longer. I'm thinking about it." Lyndee shuffled her papers into a neat stack and pushed them aside. With a twinkle in her eye, she leaned over the table, "The town news is that since Wes was run out of town, Margareet is spending her time with Billy. They say her father won't promise him anything and that her marriage will have to be based on love. Can you imagine that?"

"Lyndee, you wouldn't be gossiping, would you? It's really none of our business. My opinion is that marriage should always be based on love; but, in the end, I guess we all learn our lessons. Speaking of which, let's get these lessons finished before Langley gets here."

"Okay, okay! You're always pushing me around...but I like it," Lyndee teased and they both went back to work.

*****

Langley stepped inside the Winters' house. Straightening his tie and coat, he waited patiently on the landing for Lyndee. His eyes lit up when Lyndee approached the entrance.

"You're beautiful, Lyndee. You didn't have to dress up for me, but thank you for taking the time. Even though I don't know how you could mess with perfection. I thought we'd just go for a walk tonight. I hope you didn't have anything else planned."

Lyndee's cheeks flushed, "I always try to look my best, especially when it comes to you. A walk sounds fine to me."

"You're quite the charmer, Lyndee. I'd be interested in finding out what other talents you might possess. You should get a wrap, though; it's getting cool out, and the sun will be down soon."

"Just give me one minute and I'll get my shawl. Promise me you'll stay right there," Lyndee jokingly stated, pointing to a spot on the landing.

"You have my word. As a matter of fact, I stand on it." Langley smiled and moved to the spot she had pointed out. He watched as Lyndee giggled and scooted up the stairs. He watched her skirts and long curly red hair flying behind her. She was breathtaking. Just in the small amount of time he had spent with her, he knew she could take the worst day that he could have and make it right.

"Got it," she said, wrapping it around her shoulders. "Follow me; we'll take the trail that leads to the pond. I'll show you the swing Uncle Hank hung there years ago for us kids. It hangs on an old oak tree that stands near the water. We can swing and enjoy all the beautiful colors of fall. It will be lovely." Lyndee took Langley by the hand and led a most willing companion out the door and toward the pond.

The air had grown cool, and there was a slight breeze coming from the west. Leaves the color of rust, orange, red and burnt yellow flitted to the ground, in their descent leaving the trees almost bare. The leaves crunched beneath their feet as they walked along the shore. Lyndee giggled as she purposely stepped on every fallen leaf she could find and laughed when Langley joined in on her fun.

The breeze had kicked up to a strong wind and lifted Lyndee's hair against her face. She grabbed up her skirts and raced off to the swing with Langley in close pursuit. They stopped at the swing and Langley reached out and softly pushed Lyndee's hair from her face.

"Since you've been here, I have enjoyed every minute that we've spent together. You've made me so happy. I don't think that's a coincidence. I think it's fate and God. I believe God brought you here to Butte, Montana, for me." Langley gathered Lyndee's hands in his and then knelt down in the fallen leaves.

"I've never asked anything of anyone in my life. There is nothing that I have ever wanted that I couldn't pay for, but love is different. I've found that you can't buy it; you can only feel it. I never knew love and thought I would never love anyone. God showed me how to love by loving me. It is with that love that I can truly love you. Before I knew the Lord, I wasn't worth much, even with all the money I had. God gave me a reason and a purpose, and he brought the most beautiful woman into my life. For the first time in my life I want to share everything that I have with her, and I'm hoping she'll consent to be my wife. You must forgive me, Lyndee, for going on and on; but I've never done this before. Lyndee, will you marry me?"

For the first time in her life, Lyndee was shocked into quietness. She looked lovingly down at Langley and knew she had only one answer.

"Yes, Langley, I will marry you." Lyndee saw a changed man before her. She knew that only God can change a heart, and he had changed Langley's for the better.

Langley stood up and pulled Lyndee into a tight hug. He laid his head on her hair and breathed in the freshness of it. They were quiet while they listened to all God's creatures as they settled down for the evening.

They watched in quiet awe as the sun slowly set, while holding each other for a long time in a sweet embrace. Langley would remember this moment as the second time in his life that he was happy, and it was all because he had trusted the Lord. The words of Jesus seemed to echo in the wind, "I will never leave you nor forsake you," and Langley trusted it.

Chapter Thirty-Seven

"I can't believe that Langley proposed so quickly. He didn't even know her that long," Casey said, somewhat perplexed. It had surprised the whole family when Lyndee and Langley came inside from their walk and made their engagement announcement. Angel had watched them in the short time Lyndee had been there and had seen how she and Langley had become inseparable.

"How long do you need to know someone before you can love them?" Angel asked. Casey looked up at the evening sky as he pondered her question.

"I don't know how long. I guess there's no written rule for emotions or feelings. Love is something you can't shut down. God gave us that emotion; it mirrors his love. Look at how wicked man has been throughout the ages, and he just keeps loving us. His word says that nothing can separate us from the love of God."

"So do you know what love feels like, Casey?"

Casey smiled down at Angel, "It makes you grin for no reason. Love makes you giddy and makes everything look brand-new. It makes you stay when you feel you should walk away. It makes you hurt when they hurt and cry when they cry. Pretty much, love makes you crazy."

"Wow, that's quite an answer. Does someone make you feel all those things?"

Casey wasn't ready to divulge that answer to Angel just yet, "Yes, there is someone that makes me feel all those things, but that's something I'll have to tell you on another day. Right now what do you say to scooting over here so you can be closer to me? Then I won't feel so lonely on this huge porch swing," Casey said, patting the space next to him. "You're going to be cold, sitting so far away from my warmth. I've got these big strong arms that God blessed me with that I promise, if they were wrapped around you just right, could take away your chill."

Angel laughed, Casey was the only one she knew that could make her blush. He held out his hand, and she slid next to him and then laughingly snuggled inside his arms. "I think I could fall asleep here."

"That's good, because I think I could hold you until you fell asleep. Of course, I don't think your papa would appreciate that, so don't nod off. God willing that the Creeks don't rise, we still have tomorrow to hold one another." Casey went to release Angel, then gently hugged her close, "Well, maybe just a little while longer," he whispered.

They both smiled contentedly and sighed. A night owl screeched overhead in the quiet of the evening, and the sounds of the crickets chirping and bullfrogs bellowing their night songs echoed in their ears. Not noticing the world around them, both Angel and Casey moved to the rhythm of the swing, both of them lost in their own thoughts.

*****

Angel was just finishing closing up the schoolhouse when Casey arrived. "It's been a long, long week, and I'm glad it's over," Angel said to Casey, as she gathered up the students' tests and materials. "And it looks like it's going to be a long weekend, especially with all these tests to grade."

"I hope you saved some time for me. I have some plans to go on a picnic on Saturday, and I was hoping you would accompany me. Are you going to be up for that?" Casey asked, putting the supplies in the wagon.

"Of course I'll make time for you, Casey. You're my best friend; how could I deny you your picnic?"

"All right then, you be ready at 9 a.m. and wear something warm. At this time of year, it will still be cool out." Casey tried to hide his excitement.

"I'll be ready and waiting just for you, and I'll bring a quilt. Maybe, if you're good, I'll even bring some sandwiches."

"What do you mean, if I'm good? I'm always good," he smirked.

"I know you try."

"You want to see me try to swing you up in the wagon?" Casey asked as he swung a giggling Angel, plopping her down playfully. He hopped in next to her, and they headed home for the weekend.

161

Morning came and with it some excitement that Angel could feel in the air. She dressed hurriedly; she still had to make sandwiches, yet look her best. She always enjoyed spending time with Casey. He had a warm personality and an intriguing smile. Whenever he pulled her into his arms, it sent her heart racing. He made her feel like she was melting. Today that would be a good thing, for just as Casey had predicted, it was cool outside; and melting only meant he was holding her close.

"Hey, gorgeous, how do you manage to look so beautiful in the morning?" Casey asked.

"I hope it's not just what's on the outside, but what God has made me on the inside that you see."

"Oh, I appreciate the inside beauty; I see that, but I'm beholding the outside beauty now."

"Will you stop that? It's only nine in the morning. Really, Casey, do you go to bed with those things on your mind?"

"No, I just go to bed thinking of you. But I'll stop for now with my compliments and save the rest for later. I don't want to use all my good stuff up early. Let me help you with those things." Casey took the basket and set it down in the back of the wagon. "I think you'll like the place I picked. It's by the lake. It's beautiful there this time of year."

Climbing up into the wagon, their mood turned contemplative; and they were quiet for the rest of the ride. Angel was enjoying the scenery, but Casey had other things on his mind. He was praying the Lord would give him the right words to win Angel's heart forever.

When they arrived at the picnic spot, Casey spread out the quilt on the ground and placed the baskets next to it. Angel sat down, and then Casey sat next to her. He lay back on the blanket and stretched out in the morning sun. He noted the sun's rays filtering through the last of the leaves that had managed to hang on and survive the wind on this cool fall morning.

"You know, it's a little early for a picnic. It's actually breakfast time, so I brought egg sandwiches and some bacon. I hope you like them." Angel lifted the food out of the basket and placed it on a napkin.

162

"I've eaten your cooking before, and I haven't died yet. I'm teasing; I know it'll taste good." Casey paused and gathered the words he had been preparing, "Angel, you asked me the other day if there was anyone that made me feel like I was in love? There is someone."

Angel's heart stopped in its tracks. "Please, God," she prayed, "let me handle this like a grown-up child of yours. You know I couldn't bear to hear another girl's name on his lips other than mine, Father. Your will be done, not mine, for our lives are in your hands."

"So don't keep me guessing. Who is it that makes your heart quiver?" She held her breath, anxiously waiting for his answer.

Casey sat up and, putting his hand inside the right breast pocket of his jacket, he continued, "Ever since I was a little boy, I grew up with the best friend I ever had. She lived on the ranch my pa worked. I'd run to her house every morning, just to see her face. It was the perfect start to my day. Then I'd walk her home every night just to make sure her face was the last one I saw, and it would be the only face I would see in my dreams. I guess you could call her my dream girl. I've loved her all of my life." He stopped, then turning to Angel, he withdrew a small box from his pocket and held it out to her.

"My days are still that way, and I want every day from now until eternity to begin with your face being the first one I see in the morning and with you being the only girl in my dreams. Angel, I found I couldn't live one day without you being part of it. I believe God saved you from Wes and Langley and even Patrick, just for me. He knew we would complete one another, and you make me crazy."

Angel was in tears; God had heard her prayer. She had never known she meant so much to Casey, and her heart ached to think that he had ever been alone.

"Oh, Casey, why didn't you tell me you felt that way about me? For the longest time, I thought you just liked me as a friend."

Casey opened the small trinket box and held it out to her. "I had to let you live your life and find what was right for you, even if that meant it wasn't me." He paused, "Angel, will you marry me? Be my wife and make me complete."

Angel took the box with the beautiful engagement ring inside. Holding it close to her heart, she threw her arms around the best friend she had ever known, Casey Jones. She whispered his name over and over, until it became real to her.

Casey held her tightly, waiting for her answer. He gently sat her back and dried the tears that had trickled down her face. Angel placed her hands on Casey's face and drew him close.

"Yes, I will marry you, Casey; and I'll love you forever. I promise to continue making you crazy."

"Since you've come back from Boston, that's all I've wanted to hear, thank you. I'll do my best to make you happy; and I'll love you for the rest of my life and, if possible, beyond that." Both excited, Casey hurriedly placed the ring on Angel's finger; he didn't want her to get away again. With no distractions and nothing to tear their eyes from one another, they leaned in for a soft kiss. It was one of the most promising and soft kisses either of them had ever had. Satisfied and beaming, they smiled from ear to ear and happily ate their breakfast.

Chapter Thirty-Eight

"I think we have enough dresses and underclothing made," Cat said, holding up a slip and looking over at Angel. She had grown into a beautiful Godly woman, and Cat was proud of her only daughter. "Next we'll be making baby clothes."

"Stop teasing, Mama. Don't be rushing me. Let me get married first, and then we'll see about grandbabies."

"Aunt Cat, do you think Langley and I will have pretty babies? I hope they look like him." Lyndee was wistful.

"Yes, I think you will have pretty babies, and what's wrong with them looking like you, Lyndee? You're a beautiful girl; they'll be blessed to look like either one of you. After Uncle Hank picks up your momma and papa, we'll get to finish the decorations. It's going to be a beautiful wedding," Cat exclaimed, packing Angel's belongings.

She was going to miss both of the girls; but she knew in her heart, God couldn't have given them better mates. Casey and Langley were Godly men; she knew that both men followed their hearts, which followed their God. Cat quickly wiped away her tears.

"Momma, are you crying on my wedding day?"

"Yes, Angel, but it is from pure joy. You'll both excuse me now. I'm going downstairs to finish preparing the food." Before leaving, Cat pulled both of the girls into her bear hug and kissed them on the head. "I love you both, very much. You were blessings when you were born, and you'll be a blessing in my old age. Hurry now; we have lots to do." She released them, then tapped them on their backsides.

Angel stepped outside on the balcony to get a fresh breath of air when a wind lifted her skirt. Looking down from her current perch, she saw a small boy waving up to her. A strong gentle arm laid across her shoulders as a voice pointed out, "That's Zachery. You know that. You know I've had him since he left this world. He's quite mischievous and very loveable. He misses you. Maybe now you say goodbye to him."

Edith Gleason

"How can I do that?"

"He'll hear you." And the arm and voice drifted away. Angel thought of her life and all that had been happening. She had been given the opportunity to teach other children to give them a better start in life. She had helped the Irish and the Indians. She felt as if these had given her the redemption she needed for the loss of Zachary. Upon further recollection, it was God's forgiveness and the forgiving of herself that brought her the redemption she had been seeking.

Nothing would bring him back, and she knew he didn't hold her responsible either. As he turned to run, he smiled up at her and waved. In the faintest whisper that was swept up in the wind, he called, "I love you, Ainjo."

It was then she knew that the next time she would see him would be in heaven. She waved back and whispered, "I love you too, Zachary." She watched him as he frolicked and disappeared; then she turned and went back inside. Angel had a wedding to prepare for.

*****

The Winters' house was decorated outstandingly. White satin material draped the banisters. Bouquets of prairie roses with blanket flowers sat atop the banister ends. Yellow and red satin ribbons were pinned at each swoop of white satin along the rails and also along the walls that enclosed the sitting room. Each sitting chair was wrapped in a bow of white satin and placed in rows of eight by eight.

The candles in the chandelier over the top of the foyer were lit. The entrance dripped with bouquets of ribbons and flowers. At the front of the sitting room was a cross podium with a Bible laying on top, and it was opened to the first chapter of Philippians. The podium was wound with red and white satin and with a bouquet of wild flowers placed on each side. A long trail of white silk was rolled down the stairs and stopped at the front of the cross podium, where each couple would stand to unite in holy matrimony.

At 2 p.m. the guests began to arrive. Tim and Carson as ushers seated them in the sitting room. Jeanette played soft spirituals on the piano while Tim escorted Momma Cat and Papa Hank to the front row. Carson, leading Uncle Jim and Aunt Lorraine, were right behind

166

them. Mr. Jones, Casey's father, seated himself next to the Winters. When all the families were seated, Jeanette began to play the wedding march; and the attending guests stood up to watch as the grooms came in and took their places up front. The two grooms were first, then the best men, and the rest of the groomsmen standing next to one another.

Both men's attire consisted of black, long, linen suit coats with a white linen shirt, a black satin bow tie, pleated striped pants that were held up by black leather suspenders, and finished off with black shiny boots. They also each wore a white boutonnière pinned to their front pockets. Both men looked very honorable and promising. Casey and Langley both turned and faced the stairs, waiting patiently for their promised brides.

The three bridesmaids filed in, and the maids of honor took their places up front. The music paused, then started again as Papa Winters and Uncle Jim walked to the bottom of the staircase to escort their daughters to their respective grooms.

Lyndee was the first of the two brides, as she slowly took each step with confidence and caution so as not to trip on the ruffles of her dress. Her gown seemed to mimic her personality; it was made of white satin. The neckline was square with a fitted bodice that tapered into a point at her waist. Her sleeves were flounced and puffed. The skirt was full and pleated out from the waistband and fell into six gathered ruffles.

Her veil was a crown of primroses that adorned the top of her head. The bridal ensemble, like Lyndee, was full and lively, yet graceful and unique. She was gorgeous, and Langley thought so too as he held out his hand to his lovely bride with a smile anyone could've called pleased. He pulled his glowing bride close to his side.

Angel was next; she appeared to almost float as she descended the stairs and took Papa Hank's arm. Her gown was made of ivory satin. The neckline was a small v neck with a double collar. The bodice was in the shape of a vest that buttoned all the way down the entire front of her dress. Her sleeves were long with buttoned cuffs. Her dress was layered and flounced and formed a six-foot length train that floated behind her. Her veil was lace and dropped at her waist. She pulled up her hair into the bow of her veil, then encircled with a wreath of colorful flowers.

Angel was the vision of perfection, and it showed in Casey's eyes. Papa Hank placed Angel's hand in Casey's and watched as Casey pulled her close. Hank thanked the Lord for the mercy he had shown him and for providing a good, Godly man for his little girl. He released Angel to Casey and then sat down next to his own lovely wife, Caitlyn.

Casey smiled, and it deepened his dimples, making him even more handsome. His eyes misted over. He too thanked the Lord for giving him a real-life angel. He felt as if he had run a race, and Angel was his prize. She was the reason Casey was thankful he had chased after the dream of love. Angel not only would be the beautiful face that he had pictured in his dreams, but now Angel was the vision of loveliness that he would wake up to each morning.

Angel sighed softly as she stepped next to Casey. Here stood the strong, faithful man she had prayed for, ever since she had been little and learned that God would take care of all her needs. She smiled as she thought of God's sense of humor and how he had placed her future husband, Casey, next door to her for most of her life. Focusing her attention on the words the pastor was saying, she had one last thought before she said her vows, *A preacher's wife, who would've thought it?* and again Angel smiled to herself.

"Who gives these two women to these two men?" the preacher asked.

"We do." was the resounding answer from Papa and Uncle Jim, as both fathers stood and released their daughters. Angel and Lyndee then turned and faced their prospective handsome grooms. Casey and Langley had prepared a small saying for their respective brides. Langley was first as he cleared his throat. Reaching out, he took both Lyndee's hands in his.

"My dearest Lyndee, only God knew what an answer you would be to my life here in Montana. I am so undeserving of your love, but I pray with God's help I'll do my best. I'll love you with the biggest love I've ever had and try my hardest to make your life here the happiest it's ever been."

The pastor then spoke, "Do you, Lyndee Winters, take this man, Langley Williams, to be your lawfully wedded husband?"

"I do," For the first time in her life, Lyndee answered softly.

"And do you, Langley Williams, take this woman, Lyndee Winters, to be your lawfully wedded wife?"

"I do," Langley answered. The preacher looked to Casey to continue.

Casey also cleared his throat, "My dream Angel. I've always thought you should belong to me, and I had always prayed it would be true. One of the things I've learned as a pastor is to wait on God. I had to wait to see if God thought we should be together. He did, for here you are in all your beauty standing next to me. I'm so pleased and thankful you answered 'yes' to share your life with me and saw me as the man God chose for you. With our Heavenly Father's help, I promise to always do my best to take care of your needs and, most of all, to always love you. Angel, you are my blessing, my dream come true."

Casey stopped and nodded to the pastor, "Do you, Casey Jones, take this woman, Angel Winters, as your lawfully wedded wife?"

"I most definitely do," answered Casey adamantly.

The pastor smiled, then asked Angel, "And do you, Angel Winters, take this man, Casey Jones, as your lawfully wedded husband?"

"More than he knows, I do," answered Angel sweetly.

"With the power God has invested in me, I now present Mr. and Mrs. Langley Williams, and Mr. and Mrs. Casey Jones, both couples as man and wife! And what God has put together, let no man put asunder." The preacher finished to whoops and loud hoorahs from the crowd that had gathered at the ranch for a joyous ceremony. With a chorus of stomping feet from the excited crowd, both couples responded with a kiss of confirmation.

Hank hugged his beautiful wife Caitlyn, and Uncle Jim hugged his beautiful wife Lorraine. Both couples were pleased at the way the Lord had led their children's lives. Like with all weddings, it wasn't just the end of a ceremony, but the beginning of a lifetime.

Edith Gleason

Up in the Heavens a little boy with blonde curly hair lifts his hand, and it is taken and held by the Heavenly Father. The little boy points down with his chubby finger and excitedly squeals, "Look, Father, its Ainjo!" God smiles at the boy and answers, "Yes, Zachery, and she's all grown up." Slowly they turn and walk back into the clouds and fade into the distance.

God is good. Through every storm, during and after the rains, he watches over us. His eyes go to and fro upon the earth, and it is through the eyes of God that we learn to lean on him and learn to love ourselves and others. For as horrendous as storms can be to us, with God there is still life after the rains.

After the Rains

PSALMS 24:1, 2
*The earth is the Lord's, and the fullness thereof; the world, and they
that dwell therein, for he hath founded it upon the seas, and
established it upon the floods.*

The End